'The rediscovery of t[...]
be on a par with last [...]
Stoner, by John William[...]

S[...] ⸺⸺graph

'One of the joys of recent years is the translation into English of Stefan Zweig's stories. They have an astringency of outlook and a mastery of scale that I find enormously enjoyable'

Edmund de Waal,
author of *The Hare with the Amber Eyes*

'Zweig is at once the literary heir of Chekhov, Conrad, and Maupassant, with something of Schopenhauer's observational meditations on psychology thrown in'

Harvard Review

'The Updike of his day... Zweig is a lucid writer, and Bell renders his prose flawlessly'   *New York Observer*

'Zweig's writing is some of the most brilliant of the 20th century. His novellas all begin so innocently. By the time they have ended, you feel he has prised you open, played with your own sympathies, and exposed you to your own imperfect humanity'   *Independent*

'Zweig, prolific storyteller and embodiment of a vanished Mitteleuropa, seems to be back, and in a big way'

New York Times

STEFAN ZWEIG was born in 1881 in Vienna, into a wealthy Austrian-Jewish family. He studied in Berlin and Vienna and was first known as a poet and translator, then as a biographer. Zweig travelled widely, living in Salzburg between the wars, and was an international bestseller with a string of hugely popular novellas. In 1934, with the rise of Nazism, he moved to London, and later on to Bath, taking British citizenship after the outbreak of the Second World War. With the fall of France in 1940 Zweig left Britain for New York, before settling in Brazil, where in 1942 he and his wife were found dead in an apparent double suicide. Much of his work is available from Pushkin Press.

STEFAN ZWEIG

Burning Secret

*Translated from the
German by Anthea Bell*

**PUSHKIN
PRESS**

Pushkin Press
71–75 Shelton Street
London WC2H 9JQ

First published in German as *Brennendes Geheimnis* in 1913 © Atrium Press
English translation © Anthea Bell 2008
First published by Pushkin Press in 2008
This edition published in 2017

ISBN 978 1 782274 52 0

1 3 5 7 9 10 8 6 4 2

Text designed and typeset by Tetragon, London
Printed in Great Britain by the CPI Group, UK

www.pushkinpress.com

1

The Partner

T HE SHRILL WHISTLE of the locomotive sounded; the train had reached Semmering. For a moment the black carriages stood still in the silvery light of the heights up here, allowing a motley assortment of passengers to get out and others to board the train. Voices were raised in altercation, then the engine uttered its hoarse cry again and carried the black chain of carriages away, rattling, into the cavernous tunnel. Once again the pure, clear view of the landscape lay spread out, a backdrop swept clean by rain carried on a wet wind.

One of the new arrivals, a young man who drew admiring glances with his good clothes and the natural ease of his gait, was quick to get ahead of the others by taking a cab to his hotel. The horses clip-clopped uphill along the road at their leisure. Spring was in the air. Those white clouds that are seen only in May and June sailed past in the sky, a company clad all in white, still young and flighty themselves, playfully chasing over the blue firmament, hiding suddenly behind high mountains, embracing and separating again, sometimes crumpling up like handkerchiefs, sometimes fraying into shreds, and finally playing a practical joke on the mountains as they settled on their heads like white caps. Up here the wind too was restless as it shook the scanty trees, still wet with rain, so violently that they creaked slightly at the joints, while a thousand drops sprayed off them like sparks. And at times the cool scent of the snow seemed to drift down from the mountains, both sweet and sharp as you breathed it in. Everything in the air and on the earth was in movement, seething with impatience. Quietly snorting, the horses trotted on along the road, going downhill now, and the sound of their bells went far ahead of them.

The first thing the young man did on reaching the hotel was to look through the list of guests staying there. He was quickly disappointed. Why did I come? he began to ask himself restlessly. Staying up here in the mountains alone, without congenial companions, why, it's worse than being at the office. I'm obviously either too early or too late in the season. I'm always out of luck with my holidays; I never find anyone I know among the other guests. It would be nice if there were at least a few ladies; then a little light-hearted flirtation might help me to while away a week here agreeably enough.

The young man, a baron from a not particularly illustrious noble family in the Austrian civil service, where he was employed himself, had taken this little holiday without feeling any real need for one, mainly because all his colleagues were away for the spring break, and he didn't feel like making the office a present of his week off. Although he was not without inner resources, he was very gregarious by nature, which made him popular. He was welcome everywhere he went, and was well aware of his inability to tolerate solitude. He felt no inclination to be alone and avoided it as far as possible; he didn't really want to become any better acquainted with himself. He knew that, if he was to show his talents to best advantage, he needed to strike sparks off other people to fan the flames of warmth and exuberance in his heart. On his own he was frosty, no use to himself at all, like a match left lying in its box.

In downcast mood, he paced up and down the empty hotel lobby, now leafing casually through the newspapers, now picking out a waltz on the piano in the music-room, but he couldn't get the rhythm of it right. Finally he sat down, feeling dejected, looking at the darkness as it slowly fell and the grey vapours of the mist drifting out of the spruce trees. He wasted an idle, nervous hour in this way, and then took refuge in the dining-room.

Only a few tables were occupied, and he cast a fleeting glance over them. Still no luck! No one he really knew, only—he

9

casually returned a greeting—a racehorse trainer here, a face he'd seen in the Ringstrasse there, that was all. No ladies, nothing to suggest the chance of even a fleeting adventure. He felt increasingly bad-tempered and impatient. He was the kind of young man whose handsome face has brought him plenty of success in the past and is now ever-ready for a new encounter, a fresh experience, always eager to set off into the unknown territory of a little adventure, never taken by surprise because he has worked out everything in advance and is waiting to see what happens, a man who will never overlook any erotic opportunity, whose first glance probes every woman's sensuality and explores it, without discriminating between his friend's wife and the parlour-maid who opens the door to him. Such men are described with a certain facile contempt as lady-killers, but the term has a nugget of truthful observation in it, for in fact all the passionate instincts of the chase are present in their ceaseless vigilance: the stalking of the prey, the excitement and mental cruelty of the kill. They are constantly on the alert, always ready and willing to follow the trail of an adventure to the very edge of the abyss. They are full of passion all the time, but it is the passion of a gambler rather than a lover, cold, calculating and dangerous. Some are so persistent that their whole lives, long after their youth is spent, are made an eternal adventure by this expectation.

Each of their days is resolved into hundreds of small sensual experiences—a look exchanged in passing, a fleeting smile, knees brushing together as a couple sit opposite each other—and the year, in its own turn, dissolves into hundreds of such days in which sensuous experience is the constantly flowing, nourishing, inspiring source of life.

Well, there were no partners for a game here; the hunter could see that at once. And there is no worse frustration for a player of games than to sit at the green baize table with his cards in his hand, conscious of his superior skill, waiting in vain for a partner. The Baron called for a newspaper. Gloomily, he ran his eye over the newsprint, but his thoughts were sluggish, stumbling clumsily after the words like a drunk.

Then he heard the rustle of a dress behind him, and a voice, slightly irritated and with an affected accent, saying, "*Mais tais-toi donc, Edgar!*" A silk gown whispered in passing his table, a tall, voluptuous figure moved by like a shadow, and behind that figure came a pale little boy in a black velvet suit, who looked at him curiously. The couple sat down at their reserved table opposite him, the child visibly trying hard to behave correctly, an effort apparently belied by the dark restlessness in his eyes. The lady, on whom alone the young Baron's attention was bent, was very *soignée*, dressed with obvious good taste, and what was more, she was a type he liked very much, one

11

of those rather voluptuous Jewish women just before the age of over-maturity, and obviously passionate, but with enough experience to conceal her temperament behind a façade of elegant melancholy. At first he avoided looking into her eyes, and merely admired the beautifully traced line of their brows, a pure curve above a delicate nose that did in fact betray her race, but was so finely shaped that it made her profile keen and interesting. Her hair, like all the other feminine features of her generous body, was strikingly luxuriant, her beauty seemed to have become ostentatiously complacent in the self-assured certainty that she was widely admired. She gave her order in a very low voice, reproved the boy for playing with his fork—all of this with apparent indifference to the cautiously insinuating glances cast at her by the Baron, whom she did not seem to notice at all, although it was only his alert watchfulness that obliged her to exercise such careful control.

The Baron's gloomy face had suddenly brightened. Deep down, his nerves were at work invigorating it, smoothing out lines, tensing muscles, while he sat up very straight and a sparkle came into his eyes. He himself was not unlike those women who need the presence of a man if they are to exert their whole power. Only sensuous attraction could stimulate his energy to its full force. The huntsman in him scented prey. Challengingly, his eyes now sought to meet hers, which sometimes briefly returned his gaze with sparkling indecision as she looked past him, but never gave a clear, outright answer. He thought he also detected the trace of a smile beginning to play around her mouth now and then, but none of that was certain, and its very uncertainty aroused him. The one thing that did strike him as promising was her constant refusal to look him in the eye, betraying both resistance and self-consciousness, and then there was the curiously painstaking way she talked to her child, which was clearly meant for an onlooker. Her persistent façade of calm, he felt, meant in itself that she was beginning to feel troubled. He too was excited; the game had begun. He lingered over his dinner, kept his eyes on the woman almost constantly for half-an-hour, until he had traced every contour of her face, invisibly touching every part of her opulent body. Outside, oppressive darkness was falling, the forests sighed as if in childish alarm as huge rain clouds now reached grey hands out for them, darker and darker shadows made their way into the room, and its occupants seemed ever more closely drawn together by the silence. The mother's conversation with her child, he noticed, was becoming increasingly forced and artificial under the menace of that silence, and soon, he felt, it would dry up entirely. He decided to try testing the waters a little. He was the first to rise and, looking past her and at the landscape outside, went slowly to the door. Once there he quickly turned his head as if he had forgotten something—and caught her interested glance bent on him.

It attracted him. He waited in the lobby. She soon came out too, holding the boy's hand, leafed through the journals as she was passing and pointed out some pictures to the child. But when the Baron, as if by chance, came up to the table, apparently to choose a journal for himself but really to look more deeply into the moist brightness of her eyes, perhaps even strike up a conversation, she turned away, tapping her son lightly on the shoulder. "*Viens, Edgar! Au lit!*" She passed him coolly, skirts rustling. A little disappointed, the Baron watched her go. He had really expected to get to know her better this evening, and her brusque manner was a setback. But after all, her resistance was intriguing, and his very uncertainty inflamed his desire. In any case, he had found his partner, and the game could begin.

2

A Swift Friendship

W HEN THE BARON came into the lobby the next morning he saw the son of his fair unknown engaged in
earnest conversation with the two lift-boys, showing them the
illustrations in a Wild West book by Karl May. His mama was
not there; she must still be busy dressing. Only now did the
Baron really look at the child. He was a shy, awkward, nervous
boy of about twelve with fidgety movements and dark, darting
eyes. Like many children of that age, he gave the impression
of being alarmed, as if he had just been abruptly woken
from sleep and suddenly put down in strange surroundings.
His face was not unattractive, but still unformed; the struggle between man and boy seemed only just about to begin,
and his features were not yet kneaded into shape, no distinct
lines had emerged, it was merely a face of mingled pallor
and uncertainty. In addition, he was at just that awkward
age when children never fit into their clothes properly, sleeves
and trousers hang loose around their thin arms and legs, and

vanity has not yet shown them the wisdom of making the best of their appearance.

Wandering around down here in a state of indecision, the boy made a pitiful impression. He was getting in everyone's way. At one moment the receptionist, whom he seemed to be bothering with all kinds of questions, pushed him aside; at the next he was making a nuisance of himself at the hotel entrance. Obviously he wasn't on friendly terms with anyone here. In his childish need for chatter he was trying to ingratiate himself with the hotel staff, who talked to him if they happened to have time, but broke off the conversation at once when an adult appeared or there was real work to be done. Smiling and interested, the Baron watched the unfortunate boy looking curiously at everyone, although they all avoided him. Once he himself received one of those curious glances, but the boy's black eyes immediately veiled their alarmed gaze as soon as he caught them in the act of looking, and retreated behind lowered lids. This amused the Baron. The boy began to intrigue him, and he wondered if this child, who was obviously shy out of mere timidity, might not be a good go-between, offering the quickest way of access to his mother. It was worth trying, anyway. Unobtrusively, he followed the boy, who was loitering just outside the door again, caressing a white horse's pink nostrils in his childish need for affection, until yet again—he really did have back luck—the driver of the carriage told him rather brusquely to get out of the way. Now he was standing around once more, bored, his feelings hurt, with his vacant and rather sad gaze. The Baron spoke to him.

"Well, young man, and how do you like it here?" he began suddenly, taking care to keep his tone of voice as jovial as possible.

The boy went red as beetroot and looked up in alarm. He took the proffered hand almost fearfully, squirming with embarrassment. It was the first time a strange gentleman had ever struck up a conversation with him.

"It's very nice, thank you," he managed to stammer. The last two words were choked out rather than spoken.

"I'm surprised to hear that," said the Baron, laughing. "This is really a dull sort of place, particularly for a young man like you. What do you do with yourself all day?"

The boy was still too confused to answer quickly. Was it really possible that this elegant stranger wanted to talk, when no one else bothered about him? The idea made him both shy and proud. Making an effort, he pulled himself together.

"Oh, I read books, and we go for a lot of walks. And sometimes Mama and I go for a drive in the carriage. I'm supposed to be convalescing here, you see, I've been ill. So I have to sit in the sun a lot too, that's what the doctor said."

He uttered the last words with a fair degree of confidence. Children are always proud of an illness, knowing that danger makes them doubly important to the rest of their family.

"Yes, the sunlight's good for young men like you, it'll soon have you tanned and brown. All the same, you don't want to be sitting around all day. A young fellow like you should be going around in high spirits, kicking up a few larks. It looks to me as if you're too well-behaved—something of a bookworm, eh, with that big fat book under your arm? When I think what a young rascal I was at your age, coming home every evening with my trousers torn! You don't want to be *too* good, you know!"

Involuntarily, the child had to smile, and that did away with his fears. He would have liked to say something, but anything that occurred to him seemed too bold and confident in front of this amiable stranger who addressed him in such friendly tones. He had never been a forward boy, he was always rather diffident, and so his pleasure and shame now had him terribly bewildered. He longed to continue the conversation, but he couldn't think of anything to say. Fortunately the hotel's big, tawny St Bernard dog came along just then, sniffed them both, and was happy to be patted.

"Do you like dogs?" asked the Baron,

"Oh, yes, my grandmama has one at her villa in Baden, and when we're staying there he always spends all day with me. But that's just in summer, when we're visiting."

"We must have a couple of dozen dogs at home on our estate. I'll tell you what, if you're good while you're here I'll give you one of them. He's a brown dog with white ears, a young one. Would you like that?"

The child flushed red with delight. "Oh yes!" It burst out of him, warm and enthusiastic. Next moment, however, second thoughts set in. Now he sounded anxious and almost alarmed.

"But Mama would never let me. She says she won't have a dog at home because they make too much trouble."

The Baron smiled. At last the conversation had come around to Mama.

"Is your Mama so strict?"

The boy thought about it, looked up at him for a second as if wondering whether this strange gentleman was really to be trusted. He answered cautiously.

"No, Mama isn't strict. Just now she lets me do anything I like because I've been ill. Maybe she'll even let me have a dog."

"Shall I ask her?"

19

"Oh yes, please do," cried the boy happily. "Then I'm sure Mama will let me have him. What does he look like? You said white ears, didn't you? Can he fetch?"

"Yes, he can do all sorts of things." The Baron had to smile at the light he had kindled so quickly in the child's eyes. All of a sudden the boy's initial self-consciousness was gone, and he was bubbling over with the passionate enthusiasm that his timidity had held in check. It was an instant transformation: the shy, anxious child of a moment ago was now a cheerful boy. If only the mother were the same, the Baron couldn't help thinking, so passionate behind her show of diffidence! But the boy was already firing off questions at him.

"What's the dog's name?"

"Diamond."

"Diamond," the child said, crowing with delight. He was impelled to laugh and crow at every word that was spoken, intoxicated by the unexpected experience of having someone make friends with him. The Baron himself was surprised by his swift success, and decided to strike while the iron was hot. He invited the boy to go for a walk with him, and the poor child, starved of any convivial company for weeks, was enchanted by the idea. He chattered away, innocently providing all the information his new friend wanted and enticed out of him by means of small, apparently casual questions.

Soon the Baron knew all about the family, more particularly that Edgar was the only son of a Viennese lawyer, obviously a member of the prosperous Jewish middle class. And through further skilful questioning he quickly discovered that the child's mother had expressed herself far from happy with their stay in Semmering, and had complained of the lack of congenial company. He even thought he could detect, from Edgar's evasive answer to the question of whether Mama was very fond of Papa, that all was not entirely well in that quarter. He was almost ashamed of the ease with which he elicited all these little family secrets from the unsuspecting boy, for Edgar, very proud to think that what he said could interest a grown-up, positively pressed his confidences on his new friend. His childish heart throbbed with pride to be seen publicly on such close terms of friendship with a grown man—for as they walked along the Baron had laid an arm around his shoulders—and gradually forgot his own childhood, talking as freely as he would to a boy of his own age. Edgar was very intelligent, as his conversation showed: rather precocious, like most sickly children who have spent a great deal of time with adults, and was clearly highly strung, inclined to be either fervently affectionate or hostile. He did not seem to adopt a moderate stance to anything, and spoke of everyone or everything either with enthusiasm or a dislike so violent that it distorted his face, making him look almost vicious and ugly. Something wild and erratic, perhaps as a result of the illness from which he had only just recovered, gave fanatical fire to what he said, and it seemed that his awkwardness was merely fear, suppressed with difficulty, of his own passionate nature.

The Baron easily won his confidence. Just half-an-hour, and he had that hot and restless heart in his hands. It is so extraordinarily easy to deceive children, unsuspecting creatures whose affections are so seldom sought. He had only to lose himself in the past, and childish talk came to him so naturally and easily that the boy himself soon thought of him as one of his own kind. After only a few minutes, any sense of distance between them was gone. Edgar was blissfully happy to have found a friend so suddenly in this isolated place, and what a friend! All his companions in Vienna were forgotten, the little boys with their reedy voices and artless chatter, those images had been swept away by this one hour in his life! His entire passionate enthusiasm was now devoted to his new, his great friend, and his heart swelled with pride when, as the Baron said goodbye, he suggested meeting again tomorrow morning. And then his new friend waved as he walked away, just like a brother. That moment was, perhaps, the best of Edgar's life. It is so very easy to deceive children.

The Baron smiled as the boy stormed away. He had found his go-between. Now, he knew, the child would pester his mother to the point of exhaustion with his stories, repeating every single word—and he remembered, complacently, how cleverly he had woven a few compliments intended for her into the conversation, always speaking of Edgar's "beautiful Mama". He was certain that the talkative boy wouldn't rest until he had brought his friend and his mother together. He didn't have to life a finger to decrease the distance between himself and the fair unknown, he could dream happily now as he looked at the landscape, for he knew that a pair of hot, childish hands was building him a bridge to her heart.

3

Trio

T HE PLAN, as it turned out an hour later, was excel-
lent and had succeeded down to the very last detail.
When the young Baron entered the dining-room, deliber-
ately arriving a little late, Edgar jumped up from his chair,
greeted him eagerly with a happy smile, and waved. At the
same time he tugged his mother's sleeve, speaking to her
fast and excitedly, and unmistakably pointing to the Baron.
Blushing and looking embarrassed, she reproved him for his
over-exuberant conduct, but she could not avoid satisfying
her son's demands by glancing at the Baron once, which
he instantly took as his chance to give her a respectful bow.
He had made her acquaintance. She had to respond to the
bow, but from now on kept her head bent further over her
plate and was careful not to look his way again all through
dinner. Edgar, on the contrary, kept looking at him all the
time, and once even tried to call something over to the Baron's
table, a piece of bad manners for which his mother scolded

him soundly. When they had finished their meal Edgar was told it was time for him to go to bed, and there was much whispering between him and his Mama, the final outcome being that his ardent wish to go over to the other table and pay his respects to his friend was granted. The Baron said a few kind things that made the child's eyes sparkle again, and talked to him for a few minutes. But suddenly, with a skilful move of his own, he rose and went over to the other table, congratulated his slightly embarrassed fellow-guest on her clever and intelligent son, spoke warmly of the morning he had passed so pleasantly with him—Edgar was scarlet with pride and delight—and finally inquired after the boy's state of health in such detail and with so many questions that the mother was bound to answer him. And so, inevitably, they drifted into a conversation of some length, to which the boy listened happily and with a kind of awe. The Baron introduced himself, and thought that his resounding name had made a certain impression on the woman's vanity. At least, she was remarkably civil to him, although observing all decorum; she even left the table soon for the sake of the boy, as she apologetically added.

Edgar protested vigorously that he wasn't tired, he was ready to stay up all night. But his mother had already given the Baron her hand, which he kissed respectfully.

Edgar slept badly that night, full of a mixture of happiness and childish desperation. Something new had come into his existence today. For the first time he had become a part of adult life. Half-asleep, he forgot his own childhood state and felt that he too was suddenly grown up. Until now, brought up as a lonely and often sickly child, he had had few friends. There had been no one to satisfy his need for affection but his parents, who took little notice of him, and the servants. And the strength of a love is always misjudged if we evaluate it only by its immediate cause and not the stress that went before it, the dark and hollow space full of disappointment and loneliness that precedes all the great events in the heart's history. A great, unused capacity for emotion had been lying in wait, and now it raced with outstretched arms towards the first person who seemed to deserve it. Edgar lay in the dark, happy and bewildered, he wanted to laugh and couldn't help crying. For he loved this man as he had never loved a friend, or his father and mother, or even God. The whole immature passion of his early years now clung to the image of a man even whose name he had not known two hours ago.

But he was clever enough not to let the unexpected, unique nature of his new friendship distress him. What bewildered him so much was his sense of his own unworthiness, his insignificance. Am I good enough for him, he wondered, tormenting himself, a boy of twelve who still has to go to school and is sent to bed before anyone else in the evening? What can I mean to him, what can I give him? It was this painfully felt inability to find a means of showing his emotions that made him unhappy. Usually, when he decided that he liked another boy, the first thing he did was to share the few treasures in his desk with him, stamps and stones, the possessions of childhood, but all these things, which only yesterday had seemed full of importance and uncommonly attractive, now suddenly appeared to him devalued, foolish, contemptible. How could he offer such things to this new friend whom he dared not even call by his first name, how could he find a way, an opportunity to show his feelings? More and more, he felt how painful it was to be little, only half-grown, immature, a child of twelve, and he had never before hated childhood so violently, or longed so much to wake up a different person, the person he dreamed of being: tall and strong, a man, a grown-up like the others.

His first vivid dreams of that new world of adulthood wove their way into these troubled thoughts. Edgar fell asleep at last with a smile, but all the same, the memory of tomorrow's promise to meet his friend undermined his sleep. He woke with a start at seven, afraid of being late. He quickly dressed, went to his mother's room to say good morning—she was

28

startled, since she usually had some difficulty in getting him out of bed—and ran downstairs before she could ask any questions. Then he hung about impatiently until nine and forgot to have any breakfast; the only thing in his head was that he mustn't keep his friend waiting for their walk.

At nine-thirty the Baron came strolling nonchalantly up at last. Of course he had long since forgotten about the walk, but now that the boy eagerly went up to him he had to smile at such enthusiasm, and showed that he was ready to keep his promise. He took the boy's arm again and walked about in the lobby with the beaming child, although he gently but firmly declined to set out on their expedition together just yet. He seemed to be waiting for something, or at least so his eyes suggested as they kept going to the doors. Suddenly he stood up very straight. Edgar's Mama had come in, and went up to the two of them with a friendly expression, returning the Baron's greeting. She smiled and nodded when she heard about the planned walk, which Edgar had kept from her as something too precious to be told, but soon agreed to the Baron's invitation to her to join them. Edgar immediately looked sullen and bit his lip. What a nuisance that she had to come in just now! That walk had been for him alone, and if he had introduced his friend to his Mama it was only out of kindness, it didn't mean that he wanted to share him.

Something like jealousy was already at work in him when he saw the Baron speaking to his mother in such a friendly way.

So then the three of them went out walking, and the child's dangerous sense of his own importance, his sudden significance, was reinforced by the obvious interest both the adults showed in him. Edgar was almost exclusively the subject of their conversation, in which his mother expressed a rather feigned concern for his pallor and highly-strung nerves, while the Baron, smiling, made light of these ideas and praised the pleasant manners of his new "friend", as he called him. This was Edgar's finest hour. He had rights that no one had ever allowed him in the course of his childhood before. He was permitted to join in the conversation without being immediately told to keep quiet, he was even allowed to express all kinds of bold wishes which had always met with a poor reception before. And it was not surprising that his deceptive feeling of being grown up himself grew and flourished. In his happy dreams, childhood was left behind, like a garment he had outgrown and thrown away.

At lunch the Baron accepted the invitation of Edgar's increasingly friendly mother and joined them at their table. They were now all together, not sitting opposite each other, acquaintances had become friends. The trio was in full swing, and the three voices of man, woman, and child chimed happily together.

4

Into the Attack

THE IMPATIENT HUNTSMAN now felt that it was time to approach his prey. He did not like the informal, harmonious tone that they had adopted. It was all very well for the three of them to talk comfortably together, but talk, after all, was not his intention. And he knew that the element of companionship, a masquerade hiding his desire, kept delaying the erotic encounter between man and woman, depriving his words of their ardour and his attack of its fire. He did not want their conversation to make her forget his real aim, which, he felt sure, she had already understood.

It was very likely that he would not pursue his quarry in vain. She was at that crucial age when a woman begins to regret having stayed faithful to a husband she never really loved, when the glowing sunset colours of her beauty offer her one last, urgent choice between maternal and feminine love. At such a moment a life that seemed to have chosen its course long ago is questioned once again, for the last time the magic compass needle of the will hovers between final resignation and the hope of erotic experience. Then a woman is confronted with a dangerous decision: does she live her own life or live for her children? And the Baron, who had a keen eye for these things, thought he saw in her just that dangerous hesitation between the fire of life and self-sacrifice. She kept forgetting to bring her husband into the conversation. He obviously appeared to satisfy only her outer needs, not the snobbish ambitions aroused in her by an elegant way of life, and deep inside her she really knew very little about her child. A trace of boredom, appearing as veiled melancholy in her dark eyes, lay over her life and muted her sensuality. The Baron decided to move fast, but at the same time without any appearance of haste. On the contrary, he himself intended to be outwardly indifferent to this new friendship; he wanted her to court him, although in fact he was the suitor. He planned to display a certain arrogance, casting a strong light on the difference in social station between them, and he was intrigued by the idea of gaining possession of that beautiful, opulent, voluptuous body merely by means of exploiting that arrogance, outward appearances, a fine-sounding aristocratic name and cold manners.

The passionate game was already beginning to arouse him, so he forced himself to be cautious. He spent the afternoon in his room, pleasantly aware of being missed and wanted. However, his absence was not felt so much by her, his real target, as by the poor boy, to whom it was a torment. Edgar felt dreadfully lost and helpless, and kept waiting for his friend all afternoon with his own characteristic loyalty. Going out or doing something on his own would have seemed like an offence against their friendship. He wandered aimlessly around the hotel corridors, and the later it grew the fuller his heart brimmed with unhappiness. In his restless imagination he was already dreaming of an accident, or some injury that he had unwittingly inflicted, and he was close to tears of impatience and anxiety.

So when the Baron appeared at dinner that evening, he met with a joyous reception. Ignoring the admonishment of his mother and the surprise of the other guests, Edgar jumped up, ran to him and stormily flung his thin arms around the Baron's chest. "Where were you? Where have you been?" he cried, the words tumbling out. "We've been looking for you everywhere." His mother blushed at being involved in this unwelcome way, and said rather sternly, "*Sois sage, Edgar. Assieds-toi!*" (She always spoke French to him, although it was not a language that came naturally to her, and she could easily find herself on shaky ground in a conversation of any length.) Edgar obeyed, but would not stop asking the Baron questions. "Don't forget," his mother added, "that the Baron can do as he likes. Perhaps our company bores him." This time she brought herself into it on purpose, and the Baron was pleased to hear her fishing for a compliment with that reproach to her son.

The huntsman in him was aroused. He was intoxicated, excited to have found the right trail so quickly, to feel that the game was close to his gun. His eyes gleamed, the blood flowed easily through his veins, the words sprang from his lips with an effervescence that he himself could not explain. He was, like everyone of a strongly erotic disposition, twice as good, twice as much himself when he knew that women liked him, just as many actors find their most ardent vein when they sense that they have cast their spell over the audience, the breathing mass of spectators before them. He had always been a good story-teller, able to conjure up vivid images, but today he excelled himself, while now and then drinking a glass of the champagne that he had ordered in honour of this new friendship. He told tales of hunts in India in which he had taken part, as the guest of an aristocratic and distinguished English friend, cleverly choosing this subject as harmless although, on the other hand, he realized that anything exotic and naturally beyond her reach excited this woman. But the hearer whom he really enchanted with his stories was Edgar, whose eyes were bright with enthusiasm. He forgot to eat and gazed at the story-teller, drinking only the words from his lips. He had never hoped to see someone in the flesh who had known the amazing things he read about in his books: the big game hunts, the brown people, the Hindus, the terrible wheel of the juggernaut crushing thousands under its rim. Until now he had never stopped to think that such people really existed, he knew so little about those fairy-tale lands, and that moment lit a great fire in him for the first time. He couldn't take his eyes off his friend, he stared with bated breath at the hands that had killed a tiger and were now there before him. He hardly liked to ask a question, and when he did his voice was feverishly excited. His quick imagination kept conjuring up in his mind's eye the pictures that went with those stories, he saw his friend high up on an elephant with a purple cloth over it, brown men to right and left wearing gorgeous turbans, and then, suddenly, the tiger leaping out of the jungle, fangs bared, plunging its claws into the elephant's trunk. Now the Baron told an even more interesting tale of a cunning way to catch elephants, by getting old, tame beasts to lure the young, wild, high-spirited elephants into enclosures, and the child's eyes flashed. And then—Edgar felt as if a knife were suddenly coming down in front of him—Mama suddenly said, glancing at the time, "*Neuf heures! Au lit!*"

Edgar turned pale with horror. Being sent to bed is a terrible command to all children, because it means the most public possible humiliation in front of adults, the confession that they bear the stigma of childhood, of being small and having a child's need for sleep. But such shame was even more terrible at this fascinating moment, when it meant he must miss hearing such wonderful things.

"Just one more story, Mama, let me listen to one more, let me hear about the elephants!"

He was about to begin begging, but then he remembered his new dignity as a grown man. He ventured just one attempt, but his mother was remarkably strict today. "No, it's late already. You go up to bed. *Sois sage, Edgar.* I'll tell you all the Baron's stories afterwards."

Edgar hesitated. His mother usually accompanied him when he went to bed, but he wasn't going to beg in front of his friend. In his childish pride he tried salvaging this pathetic retreat by putting a gloss of free will on it.

"Well, Mama, then you must tell me everything! All about the elephants and everything else!"

"Yes, I will, my dear."

"And at once! Later this evening!"

"Yes, yes, but off you go to bed now. Off you go!" Edgar admired himself for succeeding in shaking hands with the

Baron and his Mama without going red in the face, although the sob was already rising in his throat. The Baron ruffled his hair in a friendly manner, which brought a smile to Edgar's tense face. But then he had to reach the door in a hurry, or they would have seen big tears rolling down his cheeks.

The Ghost

5

The Elephants

H IS MOTHER STAYED downstairs sitting at the table
with the Baron for a while, but they were no longer
discussing elephants and hunts. Now that the boy had left
them, a slightly sultry note and a sudden touch of awkwardness entered their conversation. Finally they went out into the
lobby and sat down in a corner. The Baron sparkled more
brilliantly than ever, she herself was a little merry after those
few glasses of champagne, and so the conversation quickly
assumed a dangerous character. The Baron could not really
be called handsome, he was merely young and looked very
masculine with his brown, mobile, boyish face and short
hair, enchanting her with his lively and almost over-familiar
movements. By now she liked to see him at close quarters, and
no longer feared his glance. But gradually a tone of audacity
crept into what he was saying, bewildering her slightly, rather
as if he were reaching out for her body, touching it and then
letting go again. There was something extraordinarily desirable

about it all that sent the blood flying to her cheeks. But then he laughed again, a light, unforced, boyish laugh which gave all these little liberties the easy appearance of childlike play. Sometimes she felt as if she ought to stop him with a curt word of reproof, but as she was naturally flirtatious she was only intrigued by those suggestive little remarks, and waited for more of them. Enchanted by the daring game, she ended up trying to emulate him. She cast him little fluttering glances full of promise, was already offering herself in words and gestures, even allowed him to come closer. She sensed the proximity of his voice, she sometimes felt his breath warmly caressing her shoulders. Like all gamblers, they forgot the time and lost themselves so entirely in ardent conversation that only when the lights in the lobby were dimmed at midnight did they come to their senses with a start.

She immediately jumped up, obeying her first impulse of alarm, and suddenly realized how daringly far she had ventured to go. She was not unaccustomed to playing with fire, but now her excited instincts felt how close this game was to becoming serious. With a shudder, she realized that she did not feel entirely sure of herself, that something in her was beginning to slide away, moving alarmingly close to the whirlpool. Her head was full of a bewildering mixture of fear, wine, and risqué talk, and a muted, mindless anxiety came over her, the anxiety she had felt several times in her life before at such dangerous moments, although never before had it been so vertiginous and violent. "Good night, good night. We'll meet tomorrow morning," she said hastily, about to run away, not so much from him as from the danger of that moment and a new, strange uncertainty in herself. But the Baron took the hand she had offered in farewell and held it with gentle force, kissing it not just once in the correct way but four or five times, his quivering lips moving from her delicate fingertips to her wrist, and with a slight frisson she felt his rough moustache tickle the back of her hand. A kind of warm, oppressive sensation flew from her hand along her veins and through her whole body. Hot alarm flared up, hammering menacingly at her temples, her head was burning, and the fear, the pointless fear now ran right through her. She quickly withdrew her hand.

"Ah, stay a little longer," whispered the Baron. But she was already hurrying away, with awkward haste that made her fear and confusion very obvious. The excitement that her partner in conversation wanted to arouse filled her now, she felt that everything in her was topsy-turvy. She was driven by her ardent, cruel fear that the man behind her might pursue and catch her, but at the same time, even as she made her escape, she already felt some regret that he didn't. At that moment, what she had unconsciously been longing for over the years might have happened, the adventure that she voluptuously liked to imagine close, although so far she had always avoided it just in time: a real, dangerous relationship, not simply a light flirtation. But the Baron had too much pride to run after her and take advantage of the moment. He was certain of victory, and would not pounce on the woman now in a weak moment when she was tipsy; on the contrary, he played fair, and was excited only by the chase and the thought of her surrender to him in full awareness. She could not escape him. The burning venom, he could see, was already running through her veins.

At the top of the stairs she stopped, one hand pressed to her fluttering heart. She had to rest for a moment. Her nerves were giving way. A sigh burst from her breast, half in relief to have escaped a danger, half in regret, but it was all confused, and she felt the turmoil in her blood only as a slight dizziness. Eyes half-closed, she groped her way to her door as if she were drunk, and breathed again when she held the cool handle. Now at last she was safe!

Quietly, she opened the door of her room—and next moment shrank back in alarm. Something or other had moved inside it, right at the back of the room in the dark. Her overstrained nerves cried out, she was about to call for help, but then she heard a very sleepy voice inside the room saying quietly, "Is that you, Mama?"

"For God's sake, what are you doing here?" She hurried over to the divan where Edgar lay curled up in a ball, just waking from sleep. Her first thought was that the child must be ill or needed help.

But Edgar, still very drowsy, said in a slightly reproachful tone, "I waited so long for you, and then I went to sleep."

"But why?"

"Because of the elephants."

"What elephants?"

Only then did she understand. She had promised the child to tell him about them this very evening, all about the hunt and the adventures. And the boy had stolen into her room, naïve and childish as he was, waiting for her to come in perfect confidence, and had fallen asleep as he waited. His extravagant behaviour made her indignant—although it was really with herself that she felt angry. She heard a soft murmur of guilt and shame within her and wanted to shout it down. "Go back to bed, you naughty boy," she cried. Edgar stared at her in surprise. Why was she so angry with him when he'd done nothing wrong? But his surprise made the already agitated woman even angrier. "Go back to your room at once," she shouted—furiously, because she felt that she was being unjust.

Edgar went without a word. He really was extremely tired, and was only vaguely aware, through the mists of sleep closing in, that his mother had not kept her promise, and wrong had been done to him in some way or other. But he did not rebel. Everything in him was muted by weariness, and then again, he was very angry with himself for going to sleep up here instead of staying awake. Just like a small child, he told himself indignantly before he fell asleep again.

For since yesterday he had hated his own condition of childhood.

6

Skirmishing

T HE BARON had slept badly. It is always risky to go to bed
after an adventure has been left unfinished; a restless
night, full of sultry dreams, soon made him feel sorry he had
not seized the moment after all. When he came down in the
morning, still in a drowsy and discontented mood, the boy ran
straight to him from some hiding place, gave him an enthusiastic
hug, and began pestering him with countless questions. He was
happy to have his great friend to himself for a minute or so
again, not to have to share him with Mama. His friend was to
tell stories to him, he insisted, just to him, not Mama any more,
because in spite of her promise she hadn't passed on the tales
of all those wonderful things. He besieged the displeased and
startled Baron, who had some difficulty in hiding his ill humour,
with a hundred childish demands. Moreover, he mingled these
questions with earnest assurances of his love, blissfully happy
to be alone again with the friend he had been looking for so
long, whom he had expected since first thing in the morning.

The Baron replied brusquely. He was beginning to feel bored by the way the child was always lying in wait for him, by his silly questions and his unwanted passion in general. He was tired of going around with a twelve-year-old day in, day out, talking nonsense to him. All he wanted now was to strike while the iron was hot and get the mother alone, and here the child's unwelcome presence was a problem. For the first time he felt distaste for the affection he had incautiously aroused, because at the moment he saw no chance of shaking off his excessively devoted little friend.

All the same, the attempt must be made. He let the boy's eager talk wash over him unheeded until ten o'clock, the time when he had arranged to go out walking with the child's mother, throwing a word into the conversation now and then so as not to hurt Edgar's feelings, although at the same time he was leafing through the newspaper. At last, when the hands of the clock had almost reached the hour, he pretended to remember something all of a sudden, and asked Edgar to go over to the other hotel for a moment and ask them there whether his father Count Grundheim had arrived yet.

Suspecting nothing, the child was delighted to be able to do his friend a service at last and ran off at once, proud of his dignity as a messenger, racing along the road so stormily that people stared at him in surprise. He was anxious to show

how nimble he could be when a message was entrusted to him. No, they told him at the other hotel, the Count had not arrived yet, and indeed at the moment wasn't even expected. He ran back with this message at the same rapid pace. But the Baron was not in the lobby any more. Edgar knocked at the door of his room—in vain! He looked in all the rooms, the music-room, the coffee-house, stormed excitedly away to find his Mama and ask if she knew anything, but she had gone out. The doorman, to whom he finally turned in desperation, told him, to his astonishment, that the two of them had left the hotel together a few minutes ago!

Edgar waited patiently. In his innocence he suspected nothing wrong. They couldn't stay out for more than a little while, he was sure, because the Baron wanted to know the answer to his message. However, time dragged on and on, hours passed, and uneasiness crept insidiously into his mind. Besides, since the day that seductive stranger had come into his guileless little life the child had been in a permanent state of tension, all on edge and confused. Every passion leaves its mark on the delicate organisms of children, as if making an impression on soft wax. Edgar's eyelids began to tremble nervously again; he was already looking paler. He waited and waited, patiently at first, then in a state of frantic agitation, and finally close to tears. But he still was not suspicious. His blind faith in his wonderful friend made him assume that there was a misunderstanding, and he was tormented by a secret fear that he might have misunderstood the Baron's message.

What seemed really strange, however, was that when they finally came back they were talking cheerfully, and showed no surprise. It was as if they hadn't particularly missed him. "We came back this way hoping to meet you, Edi," said the Baron, without even asking about the message. And when the child, horrified to think they might have been looking for him in vain, began assuring them that he had come straight back along the high street, and asked which way they would have gone instead, his Mama cut the conversation short. "Very well, that will do. Children ought not to talk so much."

Edgar flushed red with annoyance. This was her second mean, despicable attempt to belittle him. Why did she do it, why was she always trying to make him look like a child, when he was sure he wasn't one any more? Obviously she was envious of him for having such a friend, and was planning to get the Baron over to her side. Yes, and he was sure it was his mother who had intentionally taken the Baron the wrong way. But he wasn't going to let her treat him like that, as she'd soon see. He would defy her. And Edgar made up his mind not to say a word to her at their table in the dining-room; he wouldn't talk to anyone but his friend.

However, that turned out to be difficult. What he least expected happened: neither of them noticed his defiance. They didn't even seem to see Edgar himself, while yesterday he had been the central point of their threesome. They both talked over his head, joking and laughing together as if he had vanished under the table. The blood rose to his cheeks, there was a lump in his throat that choked him. With a shudder, he realized how terribly powerless he was. Was he to sit here and watch his mother take his friend away from him, the one person he loved, while he was unable to defend himself except by silence? He felt as if he must stand up and suddenly hammer on the table with both fists. Just to make them notice him. But he kept himself under control, merely laying his knife and fork down and not touching another morsel. However, they also ignored his stubborn refusal of food for a long time, and it wasn't until the next course came that his mother noticed and asked if he didn't feel well. It's so horrible, he thought, she always thinks the same thing, she asks if I don't feel well, nothing else matters to her. He answered briefly, saying he didn't want any more to eat, and she seemed satisfied with that. There was nothing, absolutely nothing he could do to attract attention. The Baron seemed to have forgotten him, or at least he never once spoke a word to him. His eyes burned worse and worse, spilled over, and he had to resort to the childish trick of raising his napkin quickly to his face before anyone could see the tears trickling down his cheeks, leaving salty moisture on his lips. He was glad when the meal was over.

During it his mother had suggested a carriage drive to the village of Maria-Schutz together. Biting his lower lip, Edgar had heard her. So she wasn't going to leave him alone with his friend for a single minute any more! However, his hatred was roused to fury only when she said to him, as they rose from table, "Edgar, you'll be forgetting all about your school work, you'd better stay in the hotel today and catch up with some of it!" Once again he clenched his little fist. She was always trying to humiliate him in front of his friend, reminding everyone in public that he was still a child, he had to go to school, he was merely tolerated in adult company. But this time her intentions were too transparent. He did not answer at all, but simply turned away.

"Oh dear, I've hurt your feelings again!" she said, smiling, and added, turning to the Baron, "Would it really be so bad for him to do an hour or so of work for once?"

And then—something froze rigid in the child's heart—the Baron, who called himself his friend, who had joked that he, Edgar, was too much of a bookworm, agreed with her. "Well, I'm sure an hour or two could do no harm."

Was it a conspiracy? Were they really both in league against him? Fury flared up in the child's eyes. "My Papa said I wasn't to do any school work while I was here. Papa wants me to get better here," he flung at them with all the pride of an invalid, desperately clutching at his father's authority. It came out like a threat. And the strangest part of it was that what he had said really did appear to discompose them both. His mother looked away and drummed her fingers nervously on the table. There was a painful silence. "Just as you say, Edi," replied the Baron at last, forcing a smile. "At least I don't have to take any examinations myself, I failed all mine long ago."

But Edgar did not smile at his joke, just scrutinized him with a longing but penetrating glance, as if trying to probe his soul. What was going on? Something had changed between them, and the child didn't know why. His eyes wandered restlessly, and in his heart a small, rapid hammer was at work, forging the first suspicion.

7

Burning Secret

W HAT'S CHANGED them so much, wondered the child, sitting opposite them in the carriage as they drove along, why aren't they the same to me as before? Why does Mama keep avoiding my eyes when I look at her? Why is he always trying to make jokes and clown about like that? They don't either of them talk to me the way they did yesterday and the day before, it's almost as if they had new faces. Mama has such red lips today, she must have painted them. I never saw her do that before. And he keeps frowning as if I'd hurt his feelings. But I haven't done anything to them, I haven't said a word that could annoy them, have I? No, I can't be the reason, because they're acting differently with each other too, they're not the same as before. It's as if they'd done something they don't like to talk about. They're not chattering away like yesterday, they're not laughing either, they're embarrassed, they're hiding something. They have a secret of some kind, and they don't want to share it with me. A secret, and I must find out what it is at any price. I know it must be the sort of thing that makes people send me out of the room, the sort of thing books are always going on about, and operas when men and women sing together with their arms spread wide, and hug and then push each other away. Somehow or other it must be the same as all that business about my French governess who behaved so badly with Papa, and then she was sent away. All those things are connected, I can feel that, it's just that I don't know how. Oh, I wish I knew the secret, I wish I understood it, I wish I had the key that opens all those doors, and I wasn't a child any more with people hiding things from me and pretending. I wish I didn't have to be deceived and put off with excuses. It's now or never! I'm going to get that terrible secret out of them. A line was dug into his brow, the slight twelve-year-old looked almost old as he sat there brooding, without sparing a glance for the landscape unfolding its resonant colours all around: the mountains in the pure green of the coniferous forests, the valleys still young with the fresh bloom of spring, which was late this year. All he saw was the couple opposite him on the back seat of the carriage, as if his intense glances, like a fishing-line, could bring the secret up from the gleaming depths of their eyes. Nothing whets the intelligence more than a passionate suspicion, nothing develops all the faculties of an immature mind more than a trail running away into the dark. Sometimes it is only a flimsy door that cuts children off from what we call the real world, and a chance gust of wind will blow it open for them.

Suddenly Edgar felt that the unknown, the great secret was closer than ever before, almost within reach, he felt it just before him—still locked away and unsolved, to be sure, but close, very close. That excited him and gave him a sudden, solemn gravity. For unconsciously he guessed that he was approaching the end of his childhood.

The couple opposite felt some kind of mute resistance before them, without guessing that it came from the boy. They felt constrained and inhibited as the three of them sat in the carriage together. The two eyes opposite them, with their dark and flickering glow, were an obstacle to both adults. They hardly dared to speak, hardly dared to look. They could not find the way back to their earlier light small-talk, they were already enmeshed too far in that tone of ardent intimacy, those dangerous words in which insidious lust trembles at secret touches. Their conversation kept coming up against lacunae, hesitations. It halted, tried to go on, but still stumbled again and again over the child's persistent silence.

That grim silence was particularly hard for his mother to bear. She cautiously looked at him sideways, and as the child compressed his lips she was suddenly startled to see, for the first time, a similarity to her husband when he was annoyed or angry. It was uncomfortable for her to be reminded of her husband just now, when she wanted to play a game with an adventure, a game of hide and seek. The child seemed to her like a ghost, a guardian of her conscience, doubly intolerable here in the cramped carriage, sitting just opposite with his watchful eyes glowing darkly beneath his pale forehead. Then Edgar suddenly looked up, just for a second. Both of them lowered their eyes again at once; she felt, for the first time in her life, that they were keeping watch on each other. Until now they had trusted one another blindly, but today something between the two of them, mother and child, was suddenly different. For the first time they began observing each other, separating their two lives, both already feeling a secret dislike that was still too new for them to dare to acknowledge it.

All three breathed a sigh of relief when the horses stopped outside the hotel. As an outing it had been a failure; they all felt that, but no one dared say so. Edgar jumped down first. His mother excused herself, saying that she had a headache, and quickly went upstairs. She felt tired and wanted to be alone. Edgar and the Baron were left behind. The Baron paid the driver of the carriage, looked at his watch, and walked towards the lobby, ignoring the boy. He went past Edgar, turning his elegant, slender back, walking with that slight, rhythmically springy gait that captivated the boy so much. Edgar had tried to imitate it yesterday. The Baron walked past him, he simply passed him by. Obviously he had forgotten the boy, leaving him there with the driver and the horses as if they had nothing to do with each other.

Something inside Edgar broke in two as he saw him pass like that—the man whom, in spite of everything, he still idolized. Desperation rose from his heart as the Baron passed by without a word, not even brushing him with his coat—and he wasn't aware of having done anything wrong. His laboriously maintained self-control gave way, the artificial burden of his new dignity slipped from his narrow shoulders, he was a child again, small and humble as he had been yesterday and for so long before that. It impelled him on against his will. With quick, unsteady steps he followed the Baron, stood in his way as he was about to go upstairs, and said in a strained voice, keeping back the tears only with difficulty:

"What have I done to you? You don't take any notice of me any more! Why are you always like that to me now? And Mama too! Why are you always trying to get rid of me? Am I in your way, or have I done something wrong, or what?"

The Baron gave a start of surprise. There was something in that voice that bewildered him and softened his heart. Pity for the innocent boy overcame him. "Oh, Edi, you're an idiot! I was in a bad mood today, that's all. And you're a good boy, I'm really fond of you." So saying he ruffled the boy's hair vigorously, but with his face half turned away to avoid seeing those large, moist, pleading, childish eyes. He was beginning to feel awkward about his play-acting. In fact he was already feeling ashamed of exploiting this child's love so ruthlessly, and that high little voice, shaken by suppressed sobs, physically hurt him.

"Upstairs you go now, Edi, we'll meet this evening and be friends again, you wait and see," he said in mollifying tones.

"But you won't let Mama send me straight up to bed, will you?"

"No, no, Edi, I won't," smiled the Baron. "So up you go now, I must dress for dinner."

Edgar went, happy for the moment. But soon the hammer in his mind started working away again. He had grown years older since yesterday; distrust, previously a stranger to him, had taken up residence in his childish breast.

He waited. This would be the test that decided it. They sat at the table together. Nine o'clock came, but still his mother did not send him to bed. He was beginning to feel uneasy. Why was she letting him stay up so long today, when she was usually so strict about it? Had the Baron told her what he wanted after all, had he given their conversation away? He was suddenly overcome by bitter regret for running round after him today with his heart so full of trust. At ten his mother suddenly rose from the table and wished the Baron goodnight. And strange to say, the Baron did not seem at all surprised by her early departure, or try to keep her there as he had before. The hammer in the child's breast was coming down harder and harder.

Now for the test. He too acted as if he suspected nothing, and followed his mother to the door without demur. But there he suddenly looked up, and sure enough, at that moment he caught her smiling at the Baron over his head. It was a glance of complicity, about a secret of some kind. So the Baron had indeed given him away. That was why she was going up early: he was to be lulled into a sense of security today so that he wouldn't be in their way again tomorrow.

"Swine," he muttered.

"What did you say?" asked his mother.

"Nothing," he said between his teeth. He had a secret of his own now. Its name was hatred, boundless hatred for both of them.

8

Silence

E DGAR WAS no longer restless. At last he was relishing a pure, clear feeling: hatred and open animosity. Now that he was certain he was in their way, being with them became a cruelly complex pleasure. He gloated over the idea of disrupting their plans, bringing all the concentrated force of his hostility to bear on them at last. He showed his teeth to the Baron first. When that gentleman came down in the morning and greeted him in passing with a hearty, "Hello there, Edi!", Edgar stayed where he was, sitting in an armchair, and just grunted a surly, "Morning", without looking up.

"Is your Mama down yet?"

Edgar was looking at the newspaper. "I don't know."

The Baron was taken aback. What was this all of a sudden?

"Got out of bed on the wrong side today, Edi, did you?" A joke always helped to smooth things over. But Edgar just cast him a scornful, "No," and immersed himself in the newspaper once more.

"Silly boy," muttered the Baron to himself, shrugging his shoulders, and he moved on. War had been declared.

Edgar was cool and courteous to his Mama too. He calmly rebuffed a clumsy attempt to send him out to the tennis courts. The faint, bitter smile on his curling lips showed that he was not to be deceived any more.

"I'd rather go for a walk with you and the Baron, Mama," he said with assumed friendliness, looking into her eyes. She obviously found it an inconvenient response. She hesitated, and seemed to be searching for something to say. "Wait for me here," she told him at last, and went in to breakfast.

Edgar waited. But his suspicions were aroused. His alert instincts were busy detecting some secret and hostile meaning in everything the two adults said. Distrustful as he now was, he became remarkably perceptive in his conclusions. So instead of waiting in the lobby as directed by his mother, Edgar decided to position himself in the street, where he could keep watch not only on the main entrance but on all the other doors of the hotel. Something in him scented deception. But they weren't going to get away from him any more. Out in the street, he took cover behind a woodpile, a useful trick learned from his books about American Indians. And he merely smiled with satisfaction when, after about half-an-hour, he actually did see his mother coming out of a side door carrying a bouquet of beautiful roses, and followed by that traitor the Baron. They both seemed to be in high spirits. Were they breathing a sigh of relief to have escaped him? Now, they thought, they were alone with their secret! They were laughing as they talked, starting down the road to the woods.

The moment had come. Edgar emerged from behind the woodpile at a leisurely pace, as if he happened to be here by mere chance. Very, very casually he went towards them, giving himself time, plenty of time, to relish their surprise. They were both taken aback, and exchanged a strange look. The boy slowly approached them, pretending to take this meeting entirely for granted, but he never took his mocking gaze off them.

"Oh, so there you are, Edi. We were looking for you indoors," said his mother at last. What a bare-faced liar she is, thought the child, but his lips did not relax. They kept the secret of his hatred fenced in behind his teeth.

Then they all three stood there, undecided. Each was watching the others. "Oh, let's be off," said Edgar's mother, irritated but resigned, plucking at one of the beautiful roses. Once again he saw that slight fluttering of the nostrils that betrayed her anger. Edgar stopped as if all this were nothing to do with him, looked up at the sky, waited until they had begun walking, and then set off to follow them.

The Baron made one more attempt. "It's the tennis tournament today. Have you ever seen one of those?"

Edgar looked at him with scorn. He did not even reply, just pursed his lips as if he were about to whistle. That was all his answer. His animosity was showing itself.

His unwanted presence now weighed on the other two like a nightmare. They walked as convicts walk behind their jailer, with fists surreptitiously clenched. The child wasn't really doing anything, but with every passing minute he became more intolerable to them—he and his watchful gaze, wet as his eyes were with tears grimly suppressed, his resentful ill humour, the way he rejected all attempts at conciliation with a growl.

"Go on ahead," said his mother, suddenly angry, and made uneasy by his constant close attention. "Don't keep dancing about in front of my feet like that, it makes me nervous."

Edgar obeyed, but after every few steps he turned and stood there waiting for them if they had lagged behind, his gaze circling around them like Mephistopheles in the shape of the black dog, spinning a fiery web of hostility and entangling them hopelessly in it.

His malice and silence corroded their good humour like acid, his gaze soured their conversation. The Baron dared not utter another word of gallantry, he felt with annoyance that the woman was slipping away from him again, and the flames of passion that he had so laboriously fanned were cooling again in her fear of that irritating, horrible child. They kept trying to converse, and their exchanges kept dying away. In the end, they were all three marching along the path in silence, a silence unbroken except by the rustling whisper of the trees and their own dragging footsteps. The child had throttled any conversation.

By now all three felt irritation and animosity. The betrayed child was delighted to realize that the helpless anger of the adults was all directed against his own existence, which they had ignored. Eyes sparkling with derision, he now and then scanned the Baron's grim face. He saw that the man was muttering curses between his teeth, and had to exercise self-control himself to keep from spitting them out at him. At the same time, with diabolical pleasure, he observed his mother's rising anger, and saw that they were both longing for some reason to turn on him, send him away, or in general render him harmless. But he offered them no chance, he had worked on his hostility for hours and he wasn't going to show any weakness now.

"Let's go back," said his mother suddenly. She felt that she wouldn't be able to stand this much longer, she must do something, must at least scream under the torture.

"What a pity," said Edgar calmly. "It's so nice here."

They both realized that the child was mocking them, but they dared not say anything. In the space of two days the little tyrant had learned to control himself expertly. Not a muscle moved in his face to betray his irony. Without a word, they walked the long way back. Edgar's mother was still in an agitated state when the two of them were alone in her room. She threw her sunshade and gloves angrily down. Edgar saw at once that her nerves were on edge, her temper was demanding release, but as an outburst was just what he wanted, he stayed in the room on purpose to provoke it. She paced about, sat down, drumming her fingers on the table, and then leaped to her feet again. "What a sight you look, going around all dirty and untidy like that! In front of other people too, it's a shame. Aren't you ashamed of yourself, at your age?"

Without a word in answer, the boy went over to the mirror to comb his hair. His silence, his obstinate cold silence and the scornful smile playing round his lips infuriated her. She could have hit him. "Go to your room!" she cried. She couldn't bear his presence any more. Edgar smiled, and went.

How they were both trembling before him now, how afraid she and the Baron were, afraid of every hour they all spent together, fearing his pitilessly hard eyes! The more uncomfortable they felt, the more satisfaction and pleasure there was for him in staring, and the more challenging was his delight.

Edgar was now tormenting the defenceless couple with all
the cruelty natural to children, which is still almost animal in
nature. The Baron was able to restrain his anger because he
still hoped to trick the boy, and was thinking only of his own
aims. But his mother kept losing control of herself. A chance
to shout at him came almost as a relief. "Don't play with your
fork," she snapped at him at table. "What a naughty boy you
are, you don't deserve to be eating with grown-ups!" Edgar
just kept smiling and smiling, his head slightly tilted to one
side. He knew that she was snapping at him in desperation,
and felt proud that she was exposing herself like that. His
glance was perfectly calm now, like a doctor's. Once he might
perhaps have been naughty in order to annoy her, but you
learn a lot when you hate, and you learn it fast. Now he said
nothing, he went on and on saying nothing, until the sheer
pressure of his silence had her at screaming-point.

His mother could bear it no longer. When the adults rose
from table and she saw that Edgar was about to follow them,
still looking as if such devotion was only to be taken for
granted, her resentment suddenly burst out. She abandoned
all caution and spat out the truth. Tormented by his insidious
presence, she reared and bucked like a horse tortured by flies.
"Why do you keep following me around like a three-year-old
toddler? I don't want you on my heels all the time. Children

don't belong with adults, remember that! Go and do something on your own for an hour or so. Read a book, do anything you like, but leave me alone! You're making me nervous, slinking around like that with your horrible hangdog look."

At last he'd wrung an admission out of her! Edgar smiled, and she and the Baron now seemed embarrassed. She turned and was about to move away, angry with herself for showing the child her annoyance. But Edgar just said coolly, "Papa doesn't want me going around here all on my own. Papa made me promise to be careful, he wanted me to stay close to you."

He emphasized the word "Papa", having noticed already that it had a certain inhibiting effect on them both. So somehow or other his father too must be part of that burning secret. Papa must have some kind of secret power over the couple, something that he himself didn't know about, for even the mention of his name seemed to cause them alarm and discomfiture. Once again they did not reply. They had laid down their arms. His mother went ahead, the Baron with her. After them came Edgar, but not humbly like a servant, instead he was harsh, stern, implacable as a jailer. Invisibly, he clinked their chains—they were rattling those chains, but they couldn't break them. Hatred had steeled his childish power; he, who didn't know the secret, was stronger than the two whose hands were bound by it.

9

Liars

BUT TIME WAS RUNNING OUT. The Baron had only
a few days left, and he wanted to make the most of
them. Resistance to the angry child's obstinacy, they both
felt, was useless, so they resorted to the last and ignoble way
out: flight, just to get away from his tyranny for an hour
or two.

"Take these letters to the post office, will you, and send
them by registered mail," Edgar's mother told him. They
were both standing in the hotel lobby while the Baron spoke
to a cabby outside.

Suspiciously, Edgar took the two letters. He had noticed a
servant delivering some kind of message to his mother earlier.
Were they hatching a plot against him after all?

He hesitated. "Where will I find you?"

"Here."

"Sure?"

"Yes."

"Mind you don't go away, though! You'll wait for me here in the lobby until I get back, won't you?" In his awareness of having the upper hand he spoke imperiously, as if giving his mother orders. Much had changed since the day before yesterday.

Then he went out with the two letters. At the door he met the Baron and spoke to him for the first time in two days. "I'm just taking two letters to the post. My Mama will wait for me here. Please don't leave before I come back."

The Baron brushed quickly past him. "No, no, we'll wait for you."

Edgar ran to the post office. He had to wait, because a gentleman in front of him had a dozen tedious questions. At last he was able to perform his errand, he ran straight back with the receipts—and arrived just in time to see his mother and the Baron driving away in the cab.

He was rigid with anger. He almost bent down to pick up a stone and throw it after them. So they'd got away from him after all, by means of a lie as mean as it was vile. He had known since yesterday that his mother told lies, but the idea that she could be shameless enough to break a downright promise destroyed the very last of his trust in her. He didn't understand anything at all about life, not now he knew that the words which he'd thought had reality behind them were just bright bubbles, swelling with air and then bursting, leaving nothing behind. What kind of terrible secret was it that drove grown-up people so far as to lie to him, a child, stealing away from him like thieves? In the books that he had read, people murdered and deceived each other to get their hands on money, or power, or kingdoms. But what was the reason here, what did those two want, why were they hiding from him, what were they trying to hide behind all their lies? He racked his brains. Dimly he felt that the secret was the bolt on the door of childhood, and once he had shot back the bolt and conquered the secret it would mean he was grown up, a man at long last. Oh, if he only knew the secret! But he couldn't think clearly any more. His burning, corrosive anger at knowing they had got away from him blurred the clarity of his vision.

He went out into the woods, and was just able to get safely into the shadows where no one would see him before bursting into storms of hot tears. "You liars, you cheats, traitors, rotters!" He had to shout the names he was calling them aloud or he would have choked. His rage and impatience, his anger, curiosity, helplessness, and the betrayal of the last few days, all repressed in his childish struggle to live up to his delusion of being an adult, now burst out and found relief in floods of weeping. It was the last fit of weeping in his childhood, the last and wildest, the last time he weakly gave himself up, like a girl, to the luxury of tears. In that hour of bafflement and rage he wept everything out of him: trust, love, belief, respect—his entire childhood.

It was a different boy who went back to the hotel. He was cool, he acted with deliberation. First he went to his room and carefully washed his face and eyes, so as not to give the pair of them the triumph of seeing his tearstains. Then he drew up his reckoning—and waited patiently, without any restlessness now.

The lobby was full when the carriage with the two runaways drew up outside. A few gentlemen were playing chess, others were reading the paper, the ladies were talking. The child had been sitting perfectly still among them, rather pale, darting glances here and there. Now, when his mother and the Baron came through the doorway, rather embarrassed to see him so suddenly, already about to stammer the excuse they had prepared in advance, he went up to them, perfectly calm and holding himself very upright, and said challengingly, "Baron, there's something I want to say to you."

The Baron was ill at ease. He felt as if he had been caught in some guilty act. "Yes, yes, later, in a moment!"

But Edgar raised his voice and said, loud and clear, so that everyone around could hear him, "I want to talk to you now.

You have acted very badly. You lied to me. You knew my Mama was waiting for me, and you…"

"Edgar!" cried his mother, seeing all eyes turn her way, and she moved towards him.

But now, seeing that she was going to drown out what he said, the child suddenly raised his voice to a high pitch and almost screeched, "I'm going to tell you again in front of everyone. You told the most dreadful lies, it's mean, it's a horrid thing to do."

The Baron stood there looking pale, people stared, some of them smiled.

His mother took hold of the child, who was trembling with agitation. "Go up to your room at once, or I'll slap you here in front of all these people," she said hoarsely.

But Edgar had calmed down again. He was sorry he had sounded so passionate. He was not pleased with himself, for he had really meant to challenge the Baron in cool tones, but his rage had overcome his intentions. Calmly now, without haste, he turned to the stairs.

"Baron, please forgive his naughty behaviour. As you know, he's a nervous child," she stammered, cast into confusion by the slightly malicious glances of the people staring at them. She hated nothing in the world more than scandal, and she knew she must preserve her composure now. So instead of taking flight at once, she first went to the receptionist, asked about any letters and other indifferent matters, and then went upstairs as if nothing had happened. But she left in her wake soft whispering and suppressed laughter.

On her way, she slowed her pace. She had always felt helpless in a difficult situation, and was genuinely afraid of this confrontation. She couldn't deny that it was her own fault, and then again she was afraid of the look in the child's eyes, that new, strange, peculiar look that paralysed and unsettled her. In her fear she decided to try the soft approach. For in a struggle, she knew, this angry child would now be stronger than she was.

Softly she opened the door. There sat the boy, calm and collected. There was no fear in the eyes he raised to her, they did not even betray curiosity. He seemed very sure of himself.

"Edgar," she began in as maternal a tone as possible, "what on earth came over you? I was ashamed of you. How can anyone be so bad-mannered—how can a child in particular speak to an adult like that? You will apologize to the Baron at once."

Edgar looked out of the window. When he said, "No," he might have been talking to the trees.

His self-confidence was beginning to disturb her.

"Edgar, what's the matter with you? You're not yourself at all. I can't make you out. You've always been such a good, clever boy, anyone could talk to you. And suddenly you act as if the devil had got into you. What do you have against the Baron? You seemed to like him very much, and he's been so kind to you."

"Yes, because he wanted to get to know you."

She felt uneasy. "Nonsense! What are you thinking of? How can you imagine any such thing?"

But at that the child flared up.

"He's a liar, he's only pretending. He does it out of mean, horrid calculation. He wanted to get to know you, that's why he was nice to me and promised me a dog. I don't know what he promised you or why he's making up to you, but he wants something from you too, Mama, you can be sure he does. Otherwise he wouldn't be so friendly and polite. He's a bad man. He tells lies. Just look at him some time, you'll see how he's always pretending. I hate him, he's a miserable liar, he's no good…"

"Oh, Edgar, how can you say such a thing?" She was bewildered, and hardly knew what to say in reply. Something inside her said that the child was right.

"He's no good, and you won't make me think anything else. You must see it for yourself. Why is he afraid of me?

Why does he keep out of my way? Because he knows I see through him, I know he's a bad man, I know what he's like!"

"How can you say such a thing, how can you say it?" Her brain seemed to have dried up, and only her bloodless lips kept stammering those phrases. Suddenly she began to feel terribly afraid, and did not know whether she feared the Baron or her child.

Edgar saw that his protestations had taken effect. He was tempted to go over to her side, to have a companion in the hatred and animosity he felt for the Baron. He went gently to his mother, hugged her, and his voice was emotional and cajoling

"Mama," he said, "you must have noticed that he doesn't have anything good in mind. He's made you quite different. You're the one who's changed, not me. He's turned you against me just so as to have you all to himself. I'm sure he'll let you down. I don't know what promise he's given you, I only know he won't keep it. You ought to beware of him. Anyone who tells lies to one person will tell lies to another too. He's a bad man, he's not to be trusted."

That voice, low and almost tearful, could have come from her own heart. Since yesterday she had had an uncomfortable feeling telling her the same, more and more urgently. But she was ashamed to admit that her own child was in the right. Like many people in such a situation, she extricated herself from the awkwardness of an overwhelming emotion by speaking roughly. She straightened her back.

"Children don't understand these things. You have no business meddling in them. You must behave better, and that's all there is to it."

Edgar's face froze again. "Just as you like," he said harshly. "I've warned you."

"So you refuse to apologize?"

"Yes."

They were standing close together, face to face. She felt that her authority was at stake.

"Then you will eat your meals up here. By yourself. And don't come down to our table again until you have apologized. I'll teach you good manners yet. You will not leave this room until I let you, is that understood?"

Edgar smiled. That sly smile seemed to have become a part of his lips. Privately, he was angry with himself. How foolish of him to have let his heart run away with him again, trying to warn her when she was a liar herself!

His mother walked out, skirts rustling, without looking at him again. She feared the cutting look in those eyes. She had felt uncomfortable with the child since sensing that he had his eyes wide open and was telling her exactly what she didn't want to know, didn't want to hear. It was terrible to her to find an inner voice, the voice of her own conscience, separated from herself and disguised as a child, going around masquerading as her own child, warning and deriding her. Until now her child had been a part of her life, an ornament, a toy, something dear and familiar, perhaps a nuisance now and then, but always going the same way as she did, keeping to the same rhythm as the current of her life. Today, for the first time, he was rebelling and defying her will. And now something like dislike would always be part of her memory of her son.

None the less, as she went down the stairs feeling rather weary, that childish voice spoke from her own heart. "You ought to beware of him." The warning would not be silenced. As she passed, she saw the glint of a mirror, and looked inquiringly into it, more and more closely, until the lips of her reflection opened in a slight smile and rounded as if to utter a dangerous word. She still heard the voice inside her, but she straightened her shoulders, as if shaking off all those invisible reservations, gave her reflection in the mirror a clear look, picked up her skirts and went downstairs with the determined mien of a gambler about to let her last gold coin roll over the gaming table, ringing as it went.

10

Tracks in the Moonlight

T HE WAITER WHO had brought Edgar supper in his room closed the door. The lock clicked behind him. The child jumped up, furious. It was obviously by his mother's orders that he was being locked in like a wild animal. Dark thoughts made their way out of him.

What's happening downstairs while I'm locked in here? What are those two talking about now? Is the secret going to come out at last, and I'll miss hearing it? Oh, that secret, I feel it all the time, everywhere, when I'm with grown-ups, they close their doors on it at night, they talk about it under their breath if I unexpectedly come into the room, that great secret, it's been so close to me for days now, right in front of me, and I still can't lay hands on it! I've done all I can to find out about it! I've stolen books out of Papa's desk drawer in the past and read them, and there were all those strange things in them, except that I didn't understand them. There must be a seal somewhere, and you just have to break the seal to find out what the secret is, perhaps it's in me or perhaps it's in other people. I asked the maid, I wanted her to explain those bits in the books, but she only laughed at me. It's horrible being a child, there's so much you want to know but you're not allowed to ask anyone, you always look so silly in front of grown-ups, as if you were stupid or useless. But I will find out the secret, I will, I feel I'll soon know it. There's part of it in my hands already, and I won't give up until I have it all!

He strained his ears to listen for anyone coming. A slight breeze was blowing through the trees outside, breaking the still reflection of moonlight among the branches into hundreds of swaying splinters.

They can't be planning anything good, or they wouldn't have thought up such miserable lies to keep me away. I'm sure they're laughing at me now, oh, I hate them, they're glad to be rid of me, but I'll have the last laugh. How stupid of me to let myself be shut up here and give them a moment's freedom, instead of sticking close and following all their movements. I know grown-ups are always careless, and they'll give themselves away. They always think we children are still little and we just go straight to sleep in the evenings, they forget that you can always pretend to be asleep and keep your ears open, you can make out you're stupid and be very clever all the same. When my aunt had that baby not so long ago they knew about it long before it came, it was only in front of me they acted all surprised, as if they hadn't guessed it was coming. But I knew about it too, because I'd heard them talking weeks before, in the evening when they thought I was asleep. And I'll surprise that horrible pair this time. Oh, if only I could see through doors and watch them while they think they're safe. Suppose I rang the bell now, would that be a good idea? Then the chambermaid would come and ask what I wanted. Or I could make a lot of noise, I could break some china, and then they'd open the door too. And I could slip out at that moment and go and eavesdrop. Or no—no, I don't want that. I don't want anyone to know how badly they treat me. I'm too proud for that. I'll pay them back tomorrow.

Downstairs a woman laughed. Edgar jumped; that could be his mother. It was all very well for her to laugh and make fun of him, he was just a helpless little boy to be locked in if he was in the way, thrown into a corner like a bundle of wet clothes. Cautiously, he leaned out of the window. No, it wasn't her, it was some high-spirited girls teasing a young man.

Then, at that moment, he saw how close his window really was to the ground below. And almost before he knew it he was thinking of jumping out, now, when they thought they were secure, and going to eavesdrop on them. He felt quite feverish with delight at this decision. It was as if he held the great, the

81

sparkling secret that was kept from children in his hands. Go on, out, out, said an urgent voice in him. It wasn't dangerous. There were no passers by below him, and he jumped. The gravel crunched slightly, but no one heard the faint sound.

During these last two days, stealing about and lying in wait had become his great pleasure in life. And he felt pleasure now, mingled with a slight frisson of alarm, as he tiptoed around the hotel, carefully avoiding the strong illumination of the lights. First, pressing his cheek cautiously to the pane, he looked through the dining-room window. Their usual table was empty. He went on spying in, moving from window to window. He dared not go into the hotel itself, for fear of unexpectedly meeting them somewhere in the corridors. They were nowhere to be seen. He was about to give up in despair when he saw two shadows in the doorway, and—he shrank back, ducking into the cover of darkness—his mother and her now inseparable companion came out. So he'd come at just the right moment. What were they talking about? He couldn't hear. They were speaking in low voices, and the wind was rustling in the trees. However, now he clearly heard a laugh, his mother's. It was a laugh that he had never heard from her before, a strangely high-pitched, nervous laugh, as if someone had tickled her. It was new and alarming to him. She was laughing, so it couldn't be anything dangerous they were hiding from him, nothing really huge and powerful. Edgar was slightly disappointed.

Why were they leaving the hotel, though? Where were they going by night, all by themselves? High above, the winds must be racing past on huge wings, for the sky, only a little while ago clear and moonlit, was dark now. Black scarves flung by invisible hands covered the moon from time to time, and then the night was so impenetrable that you could hardly see where you were going. Next moment, when the moon fought free, it was bright and clear again, and cool silver flowed over the landscape. This play of light and shade was mysterious, as intriguing as the game of revelation and concealment played by a woman. At this moment the landscape was stripping itself naked again. Edgar saw the two silhouettes on the other side of the path, or rather one silhouette, for they were as close as if some inner fear had merged them together. But where were the two of them going now? The pine trees were groaning in the wind, there was mysterious activity in the woods, as if the Wild Hunt were racing through them. I'll follow, thought Edgar, they can't hear my footsteps, not with all the noise the wind and the trees are making. And as the two figures went along the broad, well-lit road, he stayed in the undergrowth of the bank above it, hurrying quietly from tree to tree, from shadow to shadow. He followed them tenaciously and implacably, blessing the wind for drowning out his footsteps and then cursing it because it kept carrying the couple's words away from him. Just once, when he managed to catch their conversation, he felt sure he was about to discover the secret.

Down below him, the two of them walked along suspecting nothing. They felt happily alone in this wide, bewildering darkness, lost in their growing excitement. No premonition warned them that someone up among the dark bushes was following every step they took, two eyes were fixed on them with all the force of hatred and curiosity. Suddenly they stopped. Edgar immediately stopped as well, pressing close to a tree. He felt a thrill of anxiety. Suppose they turned now and reached the hotel ahead of him, suppose he couldn't get safely back to his room and his mother found it empty? Then all would be lost, they'd know he had been secretly watching them, and he could never hope to get that secret out of them. But they hesitated; there was obviously some difference of opinion. Luckily the moon was shining again, and he could see everything clearly. The Baron was pointing to a dark, narrow path going off to one side and down into the valley, where the moonlight did not fall in a broad stream as it did on the road here, but merely filtered through the undergrowth in droplets with a few direct rays of light. Why, Edgar wondered, does he want to go down there? His mother seemed to be saying no, but he, the Baron, was talking to her. Edgar could tell, from his gestures, how urgently he was pressing her to do something. The child felt afraid. What did the Baron want from his mother? Why was that bad man trying to drag her off into the darkness? Suddenly memories came to him from his books, which were the whole world to him, memories of murders and kidnappings, of dark crimes. Yes, that was it, the Baron wanted to murder her, and that was why he had kept Edgar away and lured her here on her own. Should he call for help? Cry murder? The words were already in his mouth, but his lips were dry and couldn't utter a sound. His nerves were on edge with agitation, he could hardly stand upright, he reached in his fright for something to cling to—and a twig cracked in his hands.

The couple turned in alarm and stared into the night. Edgar leaned against his tree in the dark, clutching it in his arms, his small body cowering in the shadows. All was deathly silent. But none the less, they seemed to have taken fright. "Let's turn back," he heard his mother say. She sounded anxious. The Baron, obviously uneasy himself, agreed. The couple walked back slowly, keeping very close. Their self-consciousness was lucky for Edgar. Ducking low in the undergrowth, crawling on all fours, his hands grazed and bleeding, he reached the bend in the road to the woods, and from there he ran back to the hotel as fast as he could go. He arrived out of breath, and then raced up the stairs. Fortunately the key that had locked him in was still in the lock outside the door; he turned it, ran into his room and threw himself on the bed. He had to rest for a few minutes, his heart was beating as wildly as the resonant clapper of a bell.

Then he ventured to get up, leaned against the window and waited for them to come back. It was quite a long wait. They must have been walking very, very slowly. He peered out, cautiously, for the window frame was not in the shadows. Here they came at a leisurely pace, moonlight shining on their clothes. They looked like ghosts in the greenish light, and again a not unenjoyable thrill of horror went through him: was the man really a murderer, what terrible deed had he, Edgar, just prevented by his presence? He could see their features clearly, white as chalk. There was an ecstatic expression on his mother's face that he had never seen there before; the Baron's expression, on the other hand, was harsh and sullen. No doubt because his plans had been foiled.

They were very close now. Their figures did not move apart until just before they reached the hotel. Would they look up? No, neither of them glanced at the window. You've forgotten me, thought the boy with wild inner rage, with a sense of secret triumph, but I haven't forgotten you. I expect you think I'm asleep or I don't count for anything, but you'll soon find out how wrong you are. I'm going to watch every step you take until I've got the secret out of that horrible, nasty man. I'll wreck the plot you're hatching between you. I'm not asleep.

Slowly, the couple approached the door. And now, as they went in, one after another, the silhouettes came together again, and their shadow disappeared through the lighted doorway, a single black form. Then the forecourt of the hotel lay empty in the moonlight again, like a broad snowfield.

11

The Attack

B REATHING HARD, Edgar stepped back from the window. He was shaken by horror. He had never in his life before been so close to anything so mysterious. The exciting world of his books, of adventures and suspense, that world of murder and betrayal had always, in his mind, existed on the same plane as fairy tales, close to the world of dreams, an unreal place and out of reach. But now, suddenly, he seemed to be in the middle of that terrifying world, and his whole being was shaken feverishly by such an unexpected encounter. Who *was* that man, the mysterious man who had suddenly come into their peaceful life? Was he really a murderer, always looking for out-of-the-way places, then dragging his mother off into the dark? Something dreadful seemed about to happen. He didn't know what to do. In the morning, he decided, he would either write to his father or send him a telegram. But might not the dreadful thing happen now, this very evening? His mother wasn't in her room yet, she was still with that strange and hateful man.

There was a narrow space between the inner door of his room and the outer door, which was not visible at first sight and which moved at a mere touch. The space was no larger than the inside of a wardrobe. He squeezed into that hand's breadth of darkness to listen for her footsteps in the corridor. He had made up his mind that he wasn't going to leave her alone for a moment. Now, at midnight, the corridor was empty, dimly illuminated only by a single light.

At last—those minutes seemed to him to go on for ever—he heard careful steps coming upstairs. He listened hard. The steps were not fast, like those of someone on the way to her room, but hesitant, dragging, very slow, as if she were climbing an infinitely steep and difficult path. There was whispering from time to time, and then silence. Edgar was trembling with agitation. Was it both of them, after all, was he still with her? The whispering was too far away. But the footsteps, although still hesitant, were coming closer and closer. Now he suddenly heard the hated voice of the Baron saying something in a low, hoarse voice, something he couldn't make out, and then his mother's voice, quickly contradicting him. "No, not tonight! No."

Edgar trembled. They were coming closer, and he heard everything now. Every step towards him, soft as it was, went painfully to his heart. And that voice, how ugly it sounded to him, the avid, insistent, horrible voice of the man he hated.

"Oh, don't be so cruel. You looked so beautiful this evening."

Then the other voice again. "No, I mustn't, I can't, oh, let me go."

There's so much fear in his mother's voice that the child takes fright. What does he want her to do now? Why is she frightened? They have come closer and closer, they must be right outside his door now. He stands just behind it, trembling and invisible, a hand's breadth away, protected only by the thin partition of the outer door. The voices were almost breathing in his ear.

"Come on, Mathilde, come on!" He hears his mother groan again, more faintly this time, her resistance waning. But what's all this? They have gone on in the dark. His mother hasn't gone into her room, she's passed it! Where is he taking her? Why doesn't she say any more? Has he stuffed a gag into her mouth, is he holding her by the throat and choking her? These ideas make him frantic. He pushes the door a tiny way open, his hand trembling. Now he can see them both in the dark corridor. The Baron has put his arm around his mother's waist and is leading her quietly away. She seems docile now. The Baron stops outside his own door. He's going to drag her off, thinks the horrified child, he's going to do something terrible.

With a wild movement he closes the door of his room and rushes out, following them. His mother screams as something suddenly comes racing out of the darkness towards them, she appears to have fainted away, her companion has difficulty in keeping her upright. And at that moment the Baron feels a small and not very strong fist in his face, driving his lip against his teeth, and something clawing like a cat at his body. He lets go of the alarmed woman, who quickly makes her escape, and strikes back blindly with his own fist before he realizes who it is he's fending off.

The child knows that he is weaker than his opponent, but he does not give in. At last, at last the moment has come, the moment he has wanted for so long, when he can let off steam, discharging all his betrayed love and pent-up hate. He hammers blindly at the man with his little fists, lips tightly compressed in feverish, mindless fury. The Baron himself has now recognized him, he too feels furious with this secret spy who has been embittering his life for the last few days and spoiling his game; he strikes back hard at anything he can hit. Edgar groans but does not let go or call for help. They wrestle silently and grimly for a minute in the midnight corridor. Gradually the Baron becomes aware of the ridiculous aspect of this scuffle with a boy of twelve, and takes firm hold of Edgar to fling him off. But the child, feeling his muscles lose their force and knowing that next moment he will be defeated, the loser in the fight, snaps furiously at that strong, firm hand trying to grab him by the nape of his neck. He bites. Involuntarily, his opponent utters a muted scream and lets go. The child uses that split second to take refuge in his room and bolt the door.

The midnight conflict has lasted only about a minute. No one to right or left has heard it. All is still, everything seems to be drowned in sleep. The Baron mops his bleeding hand with his handkerchief and peers anxiously into the darkness. No one was listening. Only in the ceiling does a last, restless light flicker—as if, it seems to him, with derision.

12

The Storm

W AS IT A DREAM, a dangerous nightmare? So Edgar
wondered next morning as he woke from a sleep
full of anxious confusion with his hair tousled. His head was
tormented by a dull thudding, his joints by a stiff, wooden
feeling, and now, when he looked down at himself, he was
startled to realize that he was still fully dressed. He jumped
up, staggered over to the mirror, and shrank back from his
own pale, distorted face. A red weal was swelling on his
forehead. With difficulty, he pulled his thoughts together
and now, in alarm, remembered everything, the fight in the
dark out in the corridor, his retreat to his room, and how
then, trembling feverishly, he threw himself on his bed in
his day clothes, ready for flight. He must have fallen asleep
there, plunging into a dark, overcast slumber and bad dreams
in which it all came back to him again, only in a different
and yet more terrible form, with the wet smell of fresh
blood flowing.

Downstairs, footsteps were crunching over the gravel. Voices flew up like invisible birds, and the sun shone, reaching far into the room. It must be late in the morning, but when he looked at his watch in alarm the hands pointed to midnight. In his agitation yesterday he had forgotten to wind it up. And this uncertainty, the sense that he was left dangling somewhere in time, disturbed him and was reinforced by the fact that he didn't know what had really happened. He quickly tidied himself and went downstairs, uneasiness and a faintly guilty feeling in his heart.

His Mama was sitting alone at their usual table in the breakfast-room. Edgar breathed a sigh of relief to see that his enemy wasn't there, that he wouldn't have to look at the hated face into which he had angrily driven his fist yesterday. And yet he still felt very uncertain as he approached the table.

"Good morning," he said.

His mother did not reply. She did not even look up, but stared at the landscape in the distance, her eyes curiously fixed. She looked very pale, there were slight rings round her eyes, and that give-away fluttering of her nostrils showed that she was upset. Edgar bit his lip. This silence confused him. He really didn't know whether he had hurt the Baron badly yesterday, and indeed whether she even knew about their fight in the dark. His uncertainty plagued him. But her face remained so frozen that he didn't even try to look at her, for fear her eyes, now lowered, might suddenly come to life behind their heavy lids and fix on him. He kept very still, not daring to make a sound, he very carefully picked up his cup and put it down again, looking surreptitiously at his mother's fingers as they nervously played with a spoon. They were curved into claws, as if betraying her secret fury. He sat like that for a quarter-of-an-hour with the oppressive feeling of waiting for something that didn't happen. Not a word, not a single word came to his rescue. And now that his mother rose to her feet, still without taking any notice of his presence, he didn't know what to do: should he stay sitting here at the table or follow her? Finally he too rose to his feet and meekly followed. She was still industriously ignoring him, and he kept feeling how ridiculous it was to be slinking after her like this. He took smaller and smaller steps, so as to lag further and further behind. Still without noticing him, she went into her room. When Edgar finally arrived, he faced a closed door.

What had happened? He didn't know what to make of it. Yesterday's sense of confidence had left him. Had he been in the wrong after all the night before when he mounted his attack? And were they preparing a punishment or some new humiliation for him? Something had to happen, he felt sure of it, something terrible must happen very soon. The sultry atmosphere of a coming thunderstorm stood between them, the electrical tension of two charged poles that must be released in a flash of lightning. And he carried this burden of premonition around with him for four lonely hours, from room to room, until his slender, childish neck was bowed under its invisible weight, and he approached their table at lunch, his demeanour humble this time.

"Good day," he tried again. He had to break this silence, this terrible threat hanging over him like a black cloud.

Once again his mother did not reply, once again she just looked past him. And with new fear, Edgar now felt that he was facing such a considered, concentrated anger as he had never yet known in his life. So far their quarrels had been furious outbursts more to do with the nerves than the feelings, quickly passing over and settled with a conciliatory smile. But this time, he felt, he had aroused wild emotions in the uttermost depths of his mother's nature, and he shrank from the violence he had incautiously conjured up. He could hardly swallow a morsel. Something dry was rising in his throat and threatening to choke him. His mother seemed to notice none of this. Only now, as she got to her feet, did she turn back as if casually, saying, "Come upstairs, Edgar, I have to talk to you."

It did not sound threatening, only so icily cold that Edgar shuddered at the words. He felt as if an iron chain had suddenly been laid around his neck. His defiance was crushed. In silence, like a beaten dog, he followed her up to her room.

She prolonged the agony by preserving her own silence for several minutes. Minutes during which he heard the clock striking, a child laughing, and his own heart hammering away in his breast. But she must be feeling very unsure of herself too, because she didn't look at him now while she spoke to him, turning her back instead.

"I don't want to say any more about your behaviour yesterday. It was outrageous, and I am ashamed to think of it. You have only yourself to blame for the consequences. All I will say to you now is, that's the last time you'll be allowed in adult company on your own. I have just written to your Papa to say that you must either have a tutor or be sent to a boarding-school. I am not going to plague myself with you any more."

Edgar stood there with his head bent. He sensed that this was only a prelude, a threat, and waited uneasily for the nub of the matter.

"You will now apologize immediately to the Baron." Edgar flinched, but she was not to be interrupted. "The Baron left today, and you will write him a letter. I will dictate it to you."

Edgar made another movement, but his mother was firm.

"And no arguing. Here is paper and ink. Sit down."

Edgar looked up. Her eyes were hard with her inflexible decision. He had never seen his mother like this before, so rigid and composed. Fear came over him. He sat down, picked up the pen, but bent his face low over the table.

"The date at the top. Have you written that? Leave an empty line before the salutation. Yes, like that. Dear Baron, add the surname and a comma. Leave another line. I have just heard, to my great regret—do you have that down?—to my great regret that you have already left Semmering—Semmering with a double 'm'—and so I must write you a letter to do what I intended to do in person, that is—write a little faster, you're not practising calligraphy!—that is to apologize for my behaviour yesterday. As my Mama will have told you, I am still convalescing from a serious illness, and I suffer from my nerves. I often see things in the wrong light, and then next moment I am sorry…"

The back bent over the table straightened up. Edgar turned, roused to defiance again.

"I'm not writing that, it isn't true!"

"Edgar!"

There was a threat in her voice.

"It's not true. I didn't do anything I ought to feel sorry for. I've done nothing wrong. I don't need to apologize. I only came when you called for help!"

Her lips were bloodless, her nostrils distended.

"I called for help? You're out of your mind!"

Edgar lost his temper. With a sudden movement, he jumped up.

"Yes, you did call for help! Out in the corridor last night, when he took hold of you. Let me go, that's what you said, let me go. Loud enough for me to hear it in my room."

"You're lying, I was never out in the corridor here with the Baron. He only escorted me as far as the stairs."

Edgar's heart missed a beat at this bare-faced lie. His voice failed him. He just looked at her, the pupils of his eyes glazed.

"You... you weren't in the corridor? And he... he didn't take hold of you? He wasn't dragging you along with him?"

She laughed. A cold, dry laugh. "You dreamed it."

That was too much for the child. By now he knew that grown-ups told lies, made bold excuses, spoke falsehoods that would slip through the finest net, served up cunning double meanings. But this cold, brazen denial, face to face, enraged him.

"And did I dream getting this mark on my forehead?"

"How should I know who you were fighting? But I'm not entering into any arguments with you, you'll do as you are told, and that's that!"

She was very pale, and was exerting the last of her strength to preserve her composure.

In Edgar, however, something now collapsed, some last flickering flame of trust. He couldn't grasp the fact that the truth could simply be trodden underfoot, extinguished like a burning match. Everything in him contracted, became cold and sharp, and he said viciously, wildly, "Oh, so I was dreaming, was I? About all that in the passage, and this mark? And how you two went for a walk in the moonlight last night, and he wanted to take you down that path, did I dream that too? Do you think you can shut me up in my room like a baby? I'm not as stupid as you think. I know what I know."

He stared boldly into her face, and that broke her strength: the sight of her own child's face right in front of her, distorted with hatred. Her anger burst out wildly.

"Go on with it, you'll go on writing at once. Or else…"

"Or else?…" His voice was insolent and challenging now.

"Or else I'll smack you as if you *were* a baby."

Edgar came a step closer. He only laughed mockingly.

Her hand slapped his face. Edgar cried out. And like a drowning man flailing out with his hands, nothing but a hollow roaring in his ears, red flickering light before his eyes, he struck back blindly with his fists. He felt himself hitting something soft, now he was hitting her face, he heard a scream…

That scream brought him back to his senses. Suddenly he saw himself, and was aware of the monstrous thing he had done, hitting his mother. Fear overcame him, shame and horror, a frantic need to get away from here, sink into the ground, be away, gone, not to have her looking at him any more. He rushed to the door and raced downstairs, through the hotel and along the road, he had to get away, right away, as if a slavering pack of hounds were on his heels.

13

First Insight

FURTHER ALONG THE ROAD he stopped. He had to hold on to a tree, his limbs were trembling so much in fear and emotional upheaval, his breathing was so laboured as it broke out of his overstressed chest. His horror at his own actions had been chasing him, and now it caught him by the throat and shook him as if he had a fever. What was he to do now? Where could he go? For here, in the middle of the woods so close to the hotel where he was staying, only fifteen minutes' walk away, he was overcome by a sense of desolation. Everything seemed different, more hostile, more dreadful now that he was alone with no one to help him. The trees that had rustled in such a friendly way around him yesterday suddenly looked dense and dark as a threat. And how much stranger and more unfamiliar must all that lay ahead of him be! This isolation, alone against the great, unknown world, made the child dizzy. No, he couldn't bear it yet, he couldn't yet bear to be on his own. But where could he go? He was afraid of his father, who was short-tempered, forbidding, and would send him straight back here. He wasn't going back, though, he'd sooner go on into the dangerous, alien atmosphere of the unknown. He felt as if he could never look at his mother's face again without remembering that he had hit it with his fist.

Then he thought of his grandmother, that kind, good old lady, who had spoiled him since he was tiny, had always protected him when he was threatened by discipline or injustice at home. He would hide with her in Baden until the first storm of fury had passed over, he'd write his parents a letter from there saying he was sorry. At this moment he was so humiliated by the mere thought of being all alone in the world, inexperienced as he was, that he cursed his pride—the stupid pride that a stranger had aroused in him with a lie. He wanted nothing but to be the child he had been before, obedient, patient, without the arrogance that, he now felt, had been so ridiculously exaggerated.

But how was he to get to Baden? How could he travel all that distance? He quickly reached into the little leather purse that he always carried with him. Thank goodness, the shiny new golden twenty-crown piece that he had been given for his birthday was still there. He had never been able to bring himself to spend it, but almost every day he had looked to make sure it was there, feasting his eyes on it, feeling rich,

and then always affectionately and gratefully polishing up
the coin with his handkerchief until it shone like a little sun.
But—the sudden thought alarmed him—would it be enough?
He had so often travelled by train without even thinking
that you had to pay, or wondering how much or how little
it cost. A crown or a hundred crowns? For the first time he
felt that certain facts of life had never occurred to him, that
all the many things around him, things he had held in his
hands and played with, were somehow imbued with a value
of their own, a particular significance. Only an hour ago he
had thought he knew everything; now he felt he had passed a
thousand secrets and problems by without a thought, and he
was ashamed that his poor amount of knowledge stumbled
over the first hurdle he encountered in life. He grew more
and more desperate, he took smaller and smaller steps on his
faltering way down to the station. He had so often dreamed
of flight, of storming out into life, becoming an emperor or
a king, a soldier or a poet, and now he looked diffidently at
the bright little station building and could think of nothing
but whether or not the twenty crowns would be enough
to get him to his grandmother's house. The shining tracks
stretched on into the countryside, the station was empty and
deserted. Shyly, Edgar went into the ticket office and asked at
the window in a whisper, so that no one else could hear him,

107

how much a ticket to Baden cost? A surprised face looked out from behind the dark partition, two eyes smiled at the timid child from behind a pair of glasses.

"A full fare?"

"Yes," stammered Edgar, but without any pride, rather in alarm in case it cost too much.

"Six crowns."

"I'd like one, please!"

Relieved, he pushed the shiny, much-loved coin over to the window, change clinked as it was pushed back to him, and all of a sudden Edgar felt wonderfully rich again. He had in his hand the brown piece of cardboard that promised freedom now, and the muted music of silver rang in his pocket.

The train would arrive in twenty minutes' time, so the time-table told him. Edgar withdrew into a corner. A few people were standing idle on the platform, not thinking about him, but the anxious child felt as if they were all looking at him and no one else, wondering why a child was travelling on his own, as if his flight and his crimes were written on his forehead. He heaved a sigh of relief when at last he heard the train's first whistle in the distance, and then the roar as it thundered in. The train that was to take him out into the world. As he boarded it, he saw that he had a third-class ticket. He had travelled only by first class before, and once again he felt that something had changed, that there were differences which had escaped his notice in the past. A few Italian labourers with hard hands and rough voices, carrying spades and shovels, sat opposite him and looked into space with dull eyes. They must obviously have been hard at work on the road, because some of them were tired and fell asleep in the clattering train, leaning back against the hard, dirty wood with their mouths open. They had been working to earn money, thought Edgar, but he could not imagine how much it was. All the same, he felt once more that money was something you didn't always have, something that had to be gained by some means or other. For the first time, he now realized that he took an atmosphere of comfort for granted, he was used to it, while to right and left of his existence there gaped abysses on which his eyes had never looked, going deep into the darkness. All of a sudden he understood that there were professions, there was purpose, that secrets clustered close around his life, near enough to touch, and yet they had gone ignored. Edgar learned a great deal from that single hour when he was all alone, he began to see through the windows of this cramped railway compartment and out into the open air. And quietly, in his dim apprehensions, something began to flower; it was not happiness yet, but a sense of amazement at the variety of life. He had fled out of fear and cowardice, he understood that now, but for the first time he had acted independently, had experienced something of the reality that had previously eluded him. For the first time, perhaps, he himself had become a secret to his mother and his father, just as the world had been a secret to him until now. He looked out of the window with new eyes. And he felt as if, for the first time, he was seeing reality, as if a veil had fallen away from what he saw and now showed him everything, the essence of its intentions, the secret nerve centre of its activity. Houses flew past as if blown away by the wind, and he found himself thinking of the people who lived in them, were they rich or poor, were they happy or unhappy, did they have his own longing to know everything, and were there perhaps children in there who, like himself, had only played games so far? The railwaymen standing by the tracks, waving their flags, seemed to him for the first time not, as before, just dolls and inanimate toys, placed there by indifferent chance; he understood that it was their fate, their own struggle with life. The wheels went round faster and faster, the rounded curves of the track now allowed the train to go down into the valley, the mountains looked gentler and more distant all the time, and then they reached the plain. He looked back once, to the place where they were still blue and full of shadows, distant and unattainable, and he felt as if his own childhood lay there, back in the place where the mountains slowly dissolved into the hazy sky.

14

Darkness and Confusion

B UT THEN IN BADEN, when the train stopped and Edgar found himself alone on the platform where the lights had just come on and the signals glowed red and green in the distance, sudden fear of the falling night mingled with this vivid sight. By day he had still felt safe, since there were people all around him and he could rest, sitting on a bench, or looking into shop windows. But how would he be able to bear it when the people had gone home, they all had beds and could look forward to some conversation and then a good night's sleep, while he would have to wander round on his own with his guilty conscience, lonely in a strange place? Oh, if only he could have a roof over his head, and soon too, instead of standing around a minute longer in the open air! That was his one clear thought.

He quickly walked along the familiar street, looking neither to right nor left, until at last he reached the villa where his grandmother lived. It was well situated on a broad road, but not where all eyes could see it, hidden behind the ivy and climbing plants of a well-tended garden, bright behind a cloud of green, an old-fashioned, comfortable white house. Edgar peered through the gratings like a stranger. Nothing moved in there, the windows were closed, obviously they were all in the garden at the back with guests. He was just putting his hand on the cool latch of the gate when something strange suddenly happened; all at once what he had thought for the last two hours would be so easy and natural appeared impossible. How could he go in, how could he say good evening to them, how could he bear and answer all the questions? How could he stand up to the first glance when he had to confess that he had secretly run away from his mother? And how could he possibly explain the enormity of what he had done when he himself didn't understand it now? A door opened inside the house. Instantly, he was overcome by a foolish fear that someone might come out, and he ran on without any idea where he was going.

He stopped when he came to the grounds of the spa buildings, because he saw that it was dark there and he didn't expect to meet anyone. Perhaps he could sit down in the grounds and at last, at long last think calmly, rest, and get his mind in order. He timidly went in. A couple of lanterns were lighted at the entrance, giving a ghostly, watery gleam of translucent green to the young leaves. Further on, however, when he had to go down the slope, everything lay like one great black and seething mass in the bewildering darkness of an early spring night. Edgar slipped shyly past a couple of people who sat talking or reading here in the light of the lanterns; he wanted to be alone. But he could not rest even in the shadowy darkness of the unlit paths. Everything there was full of a soft rustling and murmuring that shunned the light, and was mingled with the sound of the wind breathing through the leaves that bent to it, the crunch of distant footsteps, or the whispering of low voices in what were somehow sensual, sighing tones, a soft moan of fear, sounds that might come from human beings and animals and the restless slumbers of Nature all at once. There was dangerous unrest in the air here, covert, hidden, alarmingly mysterious, something moving underground in the woods that might be just to do with the spring season, but it alarmed the distraught child strangely.

He huddled on a bench in this deep darkness and tried to think what to tell them in the house. But all his ideas slipped away before he could seize and hold them, and against his own will all he could do was listen, listen to the muted tones and strange voices of the dark. How terrible this darkness was, how bewildering and yet mysteriously beautiful! Was the sound made by animals, or people, or just the spectral hand of the wind weaving all that rustling and cracking, all that humming and those enticing calls together? He listened. It was the wind stirring the trees restlessly but—and now he saw it clearly—people too, couples arm-in-arm, coming up from the well-lit town and enlivening the darkness with their mysterious presence. What did they want? He couldn't understand. They were not talking to each other, for he heard no voices, only footsteps crunching restlessly on the gravel, and here and there, in the clearing before him, he saw their figures move fleetingly past like shadows, but always as closely entwined as he had seen his mother and the Baron yesterday evening. So the secret, that great, shining, fateful secret was here too. He heard steps coming closer and closer now, and then a low laugh. Fear that the people who were coming might find him here overcame him, and he huddled even further back into the dark. But the couple now groping their way along the path through that impenetrable darkness did not see him. They went past, still entwined, Edgar breathed again. However, then their footsteps suddenly stopped right in front of his bench. They pressed their faces together. Edgar couldn't see anything clearly, he just heard a moan come from the woman's mouth, the man stammered hot, crazed words, and some sense of warm anticipation pierced his fears with a frisson of pleasure. They stayed like that for a moment, then the gravel crunched underfoot again as they walked on. The sound of their footsteps soon died away in the dark.

Edgar shuddered. The blood was pulsing back into his veins again, hotter and more turbulent than before. Suddenly he was unbearably lonely in this bewildering darkness, and he felt a strong, primeval need for a friendly voice, an embrace, a bright room, people whom he loved. It was as if the whole baffling darkness of this confusing night had sunk into him and was wrenching him apart.

He jumped up. He must get home, home, be at home somewhere in a lighted room, whatever it was like, in some kind of human relationship. What could happen to him, after all? If they beat him and scolded him, he wasn't afraid of anything now, not since he had felt that darkness and the fear of being alone.

His need drove him on, although he was hardly aware of it, and suddenly he was outside the villa again with his hand on the cool latch of the gate. He saw the window shining with light through all the green leaves now, saw in his mind's eye the familiar room and the people there behind every bright pane. Its very closeness made him happy, that first, reassuring sense of being near people who, he knew, loved him. And if he hesitated now it was only to heighten the pleasure of anticipation.

Then a voice behind him, startled and shrill, cried, "Edgar! Here's Edgar!"

His grandmother's maid had seen him. She hurried out to him and took his hand. The door inside was flung open, a dog jumped up at him, barking, they came out of the house with lights, he heard voices, cries of delight and alarm, a happy tumult of shouting and approaching footsteps, figures that he recognized now. First came his grandmother with her arms stretched out to him, and behind her—he thought he must be dreaming—was his mother. Red-eyed with crying, trembling and intimidated, he himself stood in the middle of this warm outburst of overwhelming emotions, not sure what to do or what to say, and not sure what he felt either. Was it fear or happiness?

15

The Last Dream

A LL WAS EXPLAINED: they had been looking for him here, they'd been expecting him for some time. His mother, terrified despite her anger by the frantic way the distressed child had rushed off, had made sure that a search was mounted for him in Semmering. Everything had been in terrible turmoil, the most alarming assumptions were rife, when a gentleman came to say that he had seen the child in the ticket office of the railway station at about three in the afternoon. They soon found out at the station that Edgar had bought a ticket to Baden, and without hesitation his mother immediately set off after him. Ahead of her she sent telegrams to Baden and to his father in Vienna, causing much emotion, and for the last two hours everything possible had been done to find the fugitive.

Now they had captured him, but without using force. In quiet triumph, he was led indoors, but strangely enough he felt that none of the harsh words they spoke touched him, because he saw joy and love in their eyes. And even that pretence, that appearance of anger lasted only a moment. Then his grandmother hugged him again, in tears, no one mentioned his wrong-doing any more, and he felt he was surrounded by wonderful loving care. The maid took his jacket off and brought him a warmer one, his grandmother asked if he was hungry, was there anything else he wanted, they questioned him and fussed around him with affectionate anxiety, and when they saw how self-conscious he felt they desisted. He felt, with pleasure, the sensation that he had despised but missed of being a child, and he was ashamed at his rebellion of the last few days, wanting to be rid of all this, to exchange it for the deceptive pleasure of his own isolation.

The telephone rang in the next room. He heard his mother's voice, caught a few words: "Edgar... back... yes, he came here... the last train," and wondered why she hadn't flown at him angrily, had just looked at him with that strangely subdued expression. His repentance grew wilder and more extravagant, and he would have liked to escape the solicitude of his grandmother and his aunt to go into the next room and ask her to forgive him, telling her very humbly, entirely of his own accord, that he wanted to be a child again and obedient. But when he quietly stood up, his grandmother asked, slightly alarmed, "Oh, where are you going?"

He stood there ashamed. They were already afraid if he so much as moved. He had frightened them all, and now they feared he would run away again. How could they understand that no one was sorrier for his flight than he was?

The table was laid, and they brought him a hastily assembled supper. His grandmother sat with him, never taking her eyes off him. She and his aunt and the maid enclosed him in a quiet circle, and he felt strangely soothed by this warmth. All that troubled him was that his mother didn't come into the room. If she could only know how sorry he was, she would surely have come in.

Then a carriage rattled up outside, and stopped in front of the house. The others were so startled that it made Edgar, too, uneasy. His grandmother went out. Loud voices flew this way and that through the darkness, and suddenly he knew that his father had arrived. Timidly, Edgar realized that he was alone in the room again now, and even that moment of isolation troubled him. His father was stern, was the only person he really feared. Edgar listened to the voices outside; his father seemed to be upset, he spoke in a loud and irritated voice. The voices of his grandmother and his mother chimed in, striking a soothing note, they obviously wanted to mollify him. But his father's voice remained hard, firm as the footsteps now approaching, coming closer and closer, they were in the next room, they were just outside the door that was now thrown open.

His father was very tall. And Edgar felt unspeakably small before him as he came in, nerves on edge and apparently really angry.

"What on earth were you thinking of, you little wretch, running away? How could you frighten your mother like that?"

His voice was angry, and his hands were working frantically. Stepping quietly, Edgar's mother had entered the room behind him. Her face was in shadow.

Edgar did not reply. He felt he ought to justify himself, but how could he say he had been deceived and beaten? Would his father understand?

"Well, don't you have a tongue in your head? What happened? You can tell me! Was there something you didn't like? You must have had a reason for running away! Did someone harm you in any way?" Edgar hesitated. The memory of it made him angry again, and he was about to voice his accusations. Then he saw—and it made his heart stand still—his mother make a strange movement behind his father's back. A movement that he didn't understand at first. But now that he looked at her there was a plea in her eyes. Very, very gently she raised her finger to her lips in the sign that requests silence.

At that, the child felt something warm, an enormous, wild delight spread through his entire body. He understood that she was giving him the secret to keep, that the fate of another human being lay on his small, childish lips. And wild, jubilant pride filled him to think that she trusted him, he was overcome by a readiness to make the sacrifice, he was willing to exaggerate his own guilt in order to show how much of a man he was. He pulled himself together.

"No, no… there wasn't any reason. Mama was very kind to me, but I was naughty, I behaved badly… and then… then I ran away because I was scared."

His father looked at him, taken aback. He had expected anything but this confession. He was disarmed, his anger gone.

"Oh, well, if you're sorry, then very well. I won't say any more about it today. I expect you'll think harder another time, won't you? Don't let such a thing ever happen again."

He stopped and looked at the boy, and now he sounded milder.

"How pale you look! But I think you've grown taller. I hope you won't play such childish pranks any more. After all, you're not a little boy now, you're old enough to see reason!"

All this time Edgar was looking at his mother. He though he saw something sparkling in her eyes. Or was it just the reflection of the light? No, it was a moist, clear light, and there was a smile around her mouth thanking him. He was sent to bed now, but he didn't mind being left alone. He had so much to think of, so much that was vivid and full of promise. All the pain of the last few days vanished in the powerful sensation of this first real experience; he felt happy in the mysterious anticipation of future events. Outside, the trees rustled under cover of dark night, but he was not afraid any more. He had lost all his impatience with life now that he knew how full of promise it was. He felt as if, for the first time, he had seen it as it was, no longer enveloped in the thousand lies of child-hood, but naked in its own dangerous beauty. He had never thought that days could be so full of alternating pain and pleasure, and he liked the idea that many such days lay ahead of him, that a whole life was waiting to reveal its secret to him. A first premonition of the rich variety of life had come to him; for the first time he thought he had understood the nature of human beings—they needed each other even when they appeared hostile, and it was very sweet to be loved by them. He was unable to think of anything or anyone with hatred, he did not regret anything, and found a new sense of gratitude even to the Baron, the seducer, his bitterest enemy, because he had opened the door to this world of his first true emotions to him.

All this was very sweet and pleasant to think of in the dark, mingling a little with images from dreams, and he was almost asleep already. But he thought the door suddenly opened and someone came in. He did not quite believe it, though, he was too drowsy to open his eyes. Then he sensed a soft face breathing close to his, caressing his own with mild warmth, and knew it was his mother kissing him and stroking his hair. He felt the kisses and her tears, gently responding to the caress, and took it only as reconciliation, as gratitude for his silence. Only later, many years later, did he recognize those silent tears as a vow from a woman past her youth that from now on she would belong only to him, her child. It was a renunciation of adventure, a farewell to all her own desires. He did not know that she was also grateful to him for rescuing her from an adventure that would have led nowhere, and that with her embrace she was handing on to him, like a legacy, the bitter-sweet burden of love for his future life. The child of that time understood none of this, but he felt that it was very delightful to be loved so much, and that through this love he was already drawn into the great secret of the world.

When she drew back her hand from him, her lips left his, and her quiet figure went away, skirts rustling, a warmth was left behind, breathing softly over his lips. And he sensed a sweet longing to feel such soft lips many times again, and be so tenderly embraced, but this mysterious anticipation of the secret he longed to know was already clouded by the shadows of sleep. Once again all the images of the last few hours passed vividly through his mind, once again the book of his youth opened enticingly. Then the child fell asleep and began to dream the deeper dream of his own life.

MORE FROM

STEFAN ZWEIG

TWO COLLECTIONS OF
HIS MOST SCINTILLATING
SHORT STORIES

STEFAN
ZWEIG

'One of the joys
of recent years is
the translation into
English of Stefan
Zweig's stories'
Edmund de Waal

Fantastic
Night

Tales of
Longing
and
Liberation

'The Updike
of his time'
New York
Observer

PUSHKIN
PRESS

STEFAN ZWEIG

'A phenomenal, heartbreaking collection'
Los Angeles Review of Books

'Zweig belongs with those masters of the novella—Maupassant, Turgenev, Chekhov'
Paul Bailey

The Invisible Collection

Tales of Obsession and Desire

PUSHKIN PRESS

HIS ONLY FINISHED NOVEL –
TENSE, POWERFUL,
DEVASTATINGLY ACUTE.

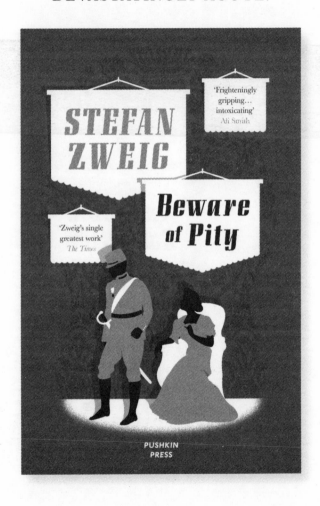

STEFAN ZWEIG

Beware of Pity

'Frighteningly
gripping…
intoxicating'
Ali Smith

'Zweig's single
greatest work'
The Times

PUSHKIN
PRESS